Patrick Deville is a novelist and French cultural attaché. He travels widely and has lived in the Middle East, Africa, south-east Asia and Latin America. He is based in Saint-Nazaire, western France, where he is the literary director of a centre for writers and translators. He is the author of nine acclaimed novels, including the bestselling *Plague and Cholera*, which was shortlisted for every major literary award in France in 2012 and won the Prix Fnac, Prix Femina and Prix des Prix.

'Garlanded with awards in his native France, Patrick Deville's fictionalised memoir of the extraordinary life of Alexandre Yersin is a remarkable testament to the man ... In mesmerising, meticulous prose, Deville paints a vivid portrait of this singular and often overlooked figure. Science has never been so exciting or thrilling'
Mail on Sunday, Novel of the Week

'Beautifully civilised and wry. Entire ethico-historical arguments may be packed into an aside. Other passing comments hint at a sweetly domesticised Borgesian metaphysics ... Delivers a surprising amount of enjoyment through its evocative images, aphor··· ···nd jokes'
Guardian

'Eloquently chronicles Ye·
tumult of the
Nature

PLAGUE
AND
CHOLERA

Patrick Deville

Translated from French
by J. A. Underwood

ABACUS

First published in Great Britain in 2014 by Little, Brown
This paperback edition published in 2015 by Abacus

1 3 5 7 9 10 8 6 4 2

Copyright © Éditions du Seuil, 2012
Translation © J. A. Underwood, 2014

The moral right of the author has been asserted.

*All characters and events in this publication, other than those
clearly in the public domain, are fictitious and any resemblance
to real persons, living or dead, is purely coincidental.*

A CIP catalogue record for this book
is available from the British Library.

ISBN 978-0-349-13953-1

Typeset in Sabon by M Rules
Printed and bound in Great Britain by
Clays, Ltd, St Ives plc

Papers used by Abacus are from well-managed forests
and other responsible sources.

 MIX
Paper from
responsible sources
FSC
www.fsc.org FSC® C104740

Abacus
An imprint of
Little, Brown Book Group
100 Victoria Embankment
London EC4Y 0DY

An Hachette UK Company
www.hachette.co.uk

www.littlebrown.co.uk

Ah, yes! – to pass into legend
On the threshold of the chattering centuries!

Jules Laforgue

Contents

last flight   1

on insects   5

Berlin   11

Paris   19

rejection   29

Normandy   33

the tall iron tower at the centre
of the world   39

ship's doctor   45

Marseilles   49

at sea   53

parallel lives   61

Albert & Alexandre   67

in flight   73

Haiphong   79

a doctor for the poor   85

the long march   91

Phnom Penh   95

a new Livingstone   103

Dalat   109

Arthur & Alexandre   115

into Sedang territory   119

Hong Kong   131

Nha Trang   141

Madagascar   147

the vaccine   151

Canton   157

Bombay   163

real life   173

Hanoi   181

the chicken controversy   189

an ark   195

an outpost of progress   199

the king of rubber   205

to posterity   215

fruit and veg   223

Vaugirard   231

machinery and implements   239

the king of quinine   245

Alexandre & Louis   251

almost a dwem   257

on the veranda   265

the ghost of the future   271

the little crowd   279

the sea   285

acknowledgements   291

last flight

The old freckled hand with the split thumb parts voile curtains. Following a sleepless night, dawn comes crimson, a
glorious cymbal-clash. The hotel room, all snow-white and
pale gold. In the distance, the four-beamed light of the tall
iron tower through a hint of mist. Below, the strikingly green
trees of square Boucicaut. The city is calm in this wartime
spring. Heaving with refugees, though. The thousands who
thought their lives had struck root. The elderly fingers, drop-
ping from the window catch, grasp the suitcase handle. Six
floors down, Yersin pushes against the gleaming wood and
shiny brass of the revolving door. A uniformed doorman
shuts the taxi door behind him. Yersin is not fleeing. He has

never fled. His seat was booked months ago in a Saigon travel agency.

The man is almost bald now, white of beard and blue of eye. The sort of jacket a gentleman farmer might wear, with beige trousers and an open-necked white shirt. Le Bourget's picture windows give onto the runway, where a parked seaplane stands on its wheels. A small white whale with a rounded belly for a dozen passengers. The gangway is being pushed against the fuselage from the left, because the early aviators, Yersin among them, were also horsemen. He is off to rejoin his little Annamites now. A scattering of would-be escapees wait on the benches of the departure lounge. In their luggage, tucked away beneath shirts and evening gowns, wads of notes and rows of ingots. German troops are at the gates of Paris. These people, wealthy enough not to collaborate, eye the clock on the wall and the watches on their wrists.

A single Wehrmacht motorcycle with sidecar would be sufficient to ground the little white whale. It is late taking off. Ignoring the tenor of the anxious conversations, Yersin jots down the odd phrase in a notebook. Up above the cockpit, where the wings meet, the propellers are seen to move. As he walks across the tarmac, the fugitives want to jostle him from behind, make him run. Those already aboard are in their seats. He is helped up the steps. Today is the last day of May '40. In the heat, the mirage of a pool of water dances on the runway. The aircraft shudders and soars into the air. Brows are mopped. This will be the last flight operated by Air France for some years. No one realises that yet.

It is also Yersin's last flight. He will never return to Paris, never again enter his room on the sixth floor of the Hôtel Lutetia. He suspects as much. Far below, the columns of the exodus heading for La Beauce. Bicycles and handcarts piled high with chairs and mattresses. Lorries at walking pace, held back by people on foot. All of them drenched by spring showers. Columns of frightened insects, fleeing the hooves of the herd. His Lutetia neighbours had all checked out. That towering beanpole of a bespectacled Irishman, Joyce in his three-piece suit, is in the Allier already. Matisse will have reached Bordeaux and be going on to St Jean de Luz. The aircraft sets course for Marseilles. Between the twin pincers of Fascism and Francoism as they close together. Meanwhile, to the north, the scorpion's tail rises, poised to strike. The 'Brown Death', France will call it.

He is familiar with both, Yersin – with both languages, both cultures, the German and the French, as well as their ancient quarrels. That other 'Death', too, he knows, the Black Death. Bubonic plague. It bears his name. Has done for forty-six years now, 'now' being the last day of May '40, when for the last time he finds himself flying over France, through its stormy sky.

Yersinia pestis.

on insects

The old man, leafing through his notebook, nods off amid the engine hum. For days he has had trouble sleeping. The hotel was awash with Passive Defence volunteers in yellow armbands. Warnings after dark. Armchairs stored safely in the basement, down galleries lined with bottles laid on their sides. Through his closed eyelids, the play of sunlight on sea. Fanny's face. A young couple's trip to Provence, down as far as Marseilles, catching insects. How can the son's story be written without the father's? The latter's was brief. The son never knew him.

In Morges in the canton of Vaud the Yersin household, like those of their neighbours, though hardly destitute, observes strict frugality. There, every penny counts. The mothers' threadbare skirts get passed down to servants. This particular father contrives, by giving private lessons, to pursue quite intensive studies in Geneva, becoming for a time a qualified secondary-school teacher with a passion for botany and entomology but subsequently, to earn a bigger crust, taking a management job in the gunpowder industry. He wears the long, close-fitting black jacket of the scientist, accompanied by a top hat. He knows all there is to know about coleopterans, specialising in *Orthoptera* and *Acrididae*.

He sketches locusts and crickets, kills them, places wing cases and antennae under the microscope, communicates with the Vaudois Natural History Society and even with the Entomological Society of France. Then he becomes 'Intendant of Powders', which is not to be sneezed at. He continues to study the nervous system of the field cricket and modernises the gunpowder industry. His forehead falls on the last of the crickets, squashing it. One arm, in a final spasm, knocks over the specimen jars. Alexandre Yersin dies aged thirty-eight. A green scarab runs across his cheek. A grasshopper becomes entangled in his hair. A Colorado beetle crawls into his open mouth. His young wife Fanny is pregnant. The boss's widow will have to leave the powdermill. The funeral over, between bundles of laundry and piles of washing-up a child is born. He is named after the dead husband.

*

On the shore of the Lake with the pure, chill water the mother buys Fig Tree House in Morges and turns it into a boarding school for girls. Fanny has style and knows how to behave. She teaches them deportment and cookery, with some painting and music on the side. The son will maintain a lifelong contempt for such activities, seeing art as a mere pastime. Painting and literature and all that crap will always remind him of the futility of the future matrons his letters refer to as the 'young bags'.

One gains the impression of a little savage, setting snares, bird-nesting, lighting fires with a magnifying glass, coming home covered in mud as if back from the battlefield or some jungle trek. The boy roams the countryside alone, swims in the Lake, builds kites. He catches insects, sketches them, transfixes them with a pin and mounts them on card. The sacrificial ritual brings the dead back to life. From his father, as warrior tribesmen hand down spear and shield, he inherits emblems, bringing the microscope and the scalpel down from a trunk in the attic. Here is a second Alexandre Yersin, a second entomologist. The dead man's collections are in a Geneva museum. It's a possible goal in life: to spend one's days in austere study, awaiting one's turn for a blood vessel to burst in the brain.

Tormenting insects aside, for generation after generation the canton of Vaud has offered little in the way of fun. The very idea is suspect. Life in these parts means atoning for the sin of living. The Yersin family performs its atonement in the shadow of the Free Evangelical Church, begotten of a schism in Lausanne, the very heart of Vaudois Protestantism. The Free Evangelical Church withholds from the state the right to pay its pastors and fund the upkeep of its places of worship. Congregations, in their destitute strictness, all but bleed themselves dry to meet their preachers' needs. It is quite another matter, keeping a Catholic priest, even one blessed with a healthy appetite. Your pastor, to please the Lord (go forth and multiply), is one who reproduces with great rapidity. Huge families fill the nest, all agape. No longer are the mothers' threadbare skirts passed down to servants. The faithful robe themselves in their elitism and probity as in togas. They are the purest of the pure, the persons most remote from material existence, the aristocrats of faith.

From this lofty coldness in the blue frigidity of Sundays, the young man, as a child, is said to have retained a brusque candour and a contempt for worldly goods. The well-behaved schoolboy (well behaved out of boredom) becomes a studious youth. The only men received in the little chintz parlour of Fig Tree House are doctor friends of his mother. Eventually it is time to choose between France and Germany and their different university systems. East of the Rhine, brilliant theoretical lectures, science passed down by learned men, professors in dark suits and celluloid collars. In Paris, clinical teaching at the patient's bedside by men in white coats, the so-called *patronal* system created by Laennec.

The choice falls on Marburg because of his mother and his mother's friends. Yersin would have preferred Berlin, but the provinces win. Fanny rents a room for her son with a worthy teacher, a prominent figure who does his sermonising at the university but is a regular churchgoer. Yersin complies, keen to cut the apron strings. To keep on the move. His dreams are those of a child. It is the beginning of a correspondence with Fanny that will end only with her death. 'When I'm a doctor I shall take you with me and we'll set up shop in the South of France or in Italy, all right?'

French becomes a secret language, truly a mother tongue, something special for the evenings, the language of his letters to Fanny.

He is twenty, and for a while his daily life will be wholly German-speaking.

Berlin

Eventually, yes, but first he must wait for a long, long year. In a letter written in July he notes that 'it is raining and cold as usual, Marburg is definitely not a sunny spot'. The teaching is as much of a disappointment to him as the climate. Yersin's mind is pragmatic, empirical, he needs to see and touch, to handle things, to build actual kites. His prominent host has features to grace a banknote. The Americans have a word for such folk: dwem. Elderly sages, white, select, learned, with goatee beards and pince-nez spectacles.

Marburg possesses four universities, a theatre, botanical gardens, law courts and a hospital. All dominated by the castle of the Landgraves of Hesse. A researcher, a writer clutching a moleskin-covered notebook, a ghost of the future on Yersin's tail, currently a guest at the Hotel Zur Sonne, climbing the steep streets in search of traces of our hero's youth, looking down on the River Lahn, has no difficulty, in this oasis of civilisation spread out beneath a low and heavy sky, in locating the tall half-timbered stone house in the dim recesses of which languishes a slight young man with sharp blue eyes and the beginnings of a beard.

The ghost, who is able to pass through walls as well as travel in time, sees behind the half-timbered façade the dark wood of the furniture, the dark leather of the armchairs and bookbindings ranged in the library. The blacks and browns of a Flemish painting. In the evening, golden lamplight for the murmured blessing, the silent meal. The pendulum catches a reflection. Higher up, it drives the gearing round by one cog, making the clock tick. On the pediment of the town hall, Death turns his sandglass to mark the hours. No one takes any notice. It is eternal, this present. The world will gain little by continuing to evolve. This civilisation has reached its peak. A few details may need to be sorted out. Some drugs could probably do with refining.

At the head of the table sits a solemn, silent Jove, Professor Julius Wilhelm Wigand, Doctor of Philosophy, Director of the Pharmaceutical Institute, Curator of the Botanic Gardens, Dean of Faculty. Each evening he receives the young Vaudois in his study. His attentions are of a paternalistic nature. He seeks to give the youth guidance in his academic rise and help him avoid mistakes. For instance, he chides him for keeping company with a man called Sternberg (the name says it all). He counsels him to join a fraternity. But then Yersin, the shy student in the armchair before him, never had a father. He has done without one up to now.

Whether reading medicine, law, botany or theology, the Marburg students of the time have one thing in common: nine out of ten belong to a fraternity. Following the initiation rites and the taking of vows, what this involves every evening is repairing to a particular watering-hole, where the walls are covered with coats of arms, to get seriously plastered and fight duels. Throats are protected with scarves, tickers with plastrons, blades are unsheathed. Fights are halted at first blood. Unshakeable friendships are born. A person will show off the scars on his body much as in later years medals will be displayed on uniforms. However, one man in ten is excluded from such camaraderie. That is the *numerus clausus* allotted to Jews under university law.

The slight young man in black opts for the tranquillity of study, country walks, discussions with Sternberg. Anatomy and clinical courses are dispensed in the lecture theatre, when these two are ready for a hospital setting. Dissection. Experiencing the real thing. In Berlin, where Yersin eventually moves, he attends two hip resections in the same week, while Marburg used to see only one a year. At last he is walking the streets of a major capital. That year, the hotels are full of diplomats and explorers. Berlin is becoming the capital of the world.

On Bismarck's initiative, all the colonial nations assemble there around the atlas to divide up Africa. The occasion, the Congress of Berlin. At which the mythical Stanley, who fourteen years earlier found Livingstone, finds himself representing the King of the Belgians, owner of the Congo. Yersin reads the newspapers, researches Livingstone's life, and the Scotsman becomes his role model: the man who is simultaneously explorer, man of action, scientist, pastor, discoverer of the Zambesi and doctor, the man who, lost for years in unknown reaches of central Africa, when Stanley finally found him again opted to stay put and died there.

One day, Yersin will be the new Livingstone.

He writes as much in a letter to Fanny.

Germany, like France and Britain, is deploying sabre and machine gun to carve itself out an empire, colonising the Cameroons, what is now Namibia, what is now Tanzania and up as far as Zanzibar. In that year of the Congress of Berlin, Arthur Rimbaud, author of a polemical pamphlet entitled *Bismarck's Dream*, hauls two thousand rifles and sixty thousand rounds of ammunition by camel train to Abyssinia for King Menelik. The former French poet turned promoter of French interests is against the territorial designs of the British and Egyptians under Gordon. 'Their Gordon is a fool, their Wolseley an ass, and all their undertakings a senseless string of absurdities and depredations.' He stresses the primary strategic significance of the port; he uses the spelling 'Dhjibouti', as Baudelaire writes 'Saharah'. He draws up an exploration report for France's Geographical Society, dispatches geopolitical articles to a Cairo newspaper (*Le Bosphore égyptien*) that find an echo in Germany, Austria and Italy. He describes the ravages of war. 'The Abyssinians, in the space of a few months, have consumed dourah supplies left by the Egyptians that might have lasted several years. Famine and plague are just around the corner.'

It is an insect that spreads bubonic plague. The flea. No one, at the time, knows this yet.

From Berlin, Yersin goes on to Jena. He buys from Carl Zeiss the very latest microscope, which will never leave him subsequently, accompanying his global travels in his baggage, the microscope that, ten years hence, will help him identify the plague bacillus. Carl Zeiss is a kind of Spinoza, and for both men polishing lenses fosters contemplation and brings Utopia closer. Baruch Spinoza was another Jew, Sternberg tells him. The two students, back in Marburg, take turns leaning over the brand-new instrument, fiddling with the notched focusing wheel to discern the geometry of a dragonfly's wing.

Yersin, too, witnesses anti-Semitic violence at first hand, shop windows being smashed, punches thrown. The word plague may well slip into the two students' conversation.

People who have had neither often confuse plague with leprosy. The great plague of medieval times, the Black Death, gives us the demographic statistic of twenty-five million dead. Half Europe's population is cut down, no war ever caused such slaughter, the Black Death attains metaphysical proportions, heralds God's wrath, brings the Chastisement. As the two students know, the Swiss were not always gentle advocates of tolerance and moderation. Five centuries earlier the people of Villeneuve on the shore of the Lake burnt Jews alive, accusing them of spreading the epidemic by poisoning wells. Five centuries on, they concede, obscurantism may have diminished but there is still as much hatred. And no more is known about plague. How it arrives, kills and goes. One day, additional knowledge may be acquired. The two students have faith in science, in progress. Curing plague would be a huge leap, Sternberg says. Yersin tells his friend he is leaving for France.

Twelve months later, he is still studying in Paris. In that year of the Congress of Berlin, as Arthur Rimbaud toils across stony deserts behind camels, Louis Pasteur has just saved the life of young Joseph Meister. Curing rabies by inoculation is the first step. Soon it will no longer be a case of choose your poison: plague or cholera; both diseases will be curable. Yersin has the advantage of being bilingual. Even bilingual himself, Sternberg might have paused. Between Berlin or Paris, as between Scylla and Charybdis. Something of a lucid pessimist, Sternberg, if that is not a pleonasm. Ten years later, at the beginning of the Dreyfus Affair, Yersin's signature will not be found on any petition. Granted, all these things, these horrors of Europe, would have given anyone a taste for the Antipodes. When the case comes to court, Yersin is in Nha Trang or Hong Kong.

Paris

When Yersin discovers the other capital, it is above all anti-Germanism that he discovers. In Paris, the spiked helmet and Bavarian songs are best avoided. Yodel instead, wearing that slightly odd Swiss hat.

Since Sedan, fifteen years earlier, France has been smaller and that does not suit it. With Alsace and Lorraine gone, the amputee has been taking revenge, conquering a vast empire overseas, far larger than Germany's. From the Caribbean isles to those of Polynesia, from Africa to Asia: just as with the Union Jack, the sun never sets on the *tricolore*. That year Pavie, the explorer of Laos, meets Brazza, explorer of the Congo. At a restaurant in Paris's rue Mazarine, in fact, La

Petite Vache, where another little crowd, the explorers known as the 'Sahariens', have taken to gathering. Two years earlier the French navy set out from its base in Cochinchina to seize the provinces of Annam and Tonkin. Yersin has read the accounts, pored over the maps. Here are men, real men such as would never stagnate in Marburg. He is sure he is making the right choice. This is where he should live.

Possibly for the last time in its history, late nineteenth-century Paris is a modern city. Its Haussmannian renovation is complete. An underground railway is planned. 'I am just off to the Louvre Museum. Today I shall be looking at Egyptian antiquities.' Yersin reads the papers in the lounge of Le Bon Marché. The Boucicaut family, who own the department store, will have the Hôtel Lutetia built opposite twenty-five years hence. And Yersin, towards the end of his life, will make a habit of staying there for several weeks in the year, having travelled halfway round the world for the purpose. Always in the corner room on the sixth floor, only a few hundred metres from his first address as a student, a mansarded slum dwelling in rue Madame from which, as he tells Fanny at the time, by twisting his neck he can glimpse one tower of St Sulpice Church.

In rue d'Ulm, Louis Pasteur has just performed a second successful anti-rabies vaccination. First the youth from Alsace, Joseph Meister; now Jean-Baptiste Jupille from the

Jura. Soon people come flocking from all over. Until now, in every stretch of snow-covered countryside and forest where wolves live, in France as in Russia, often the only treatment has been to restrain rabid animals and suffocate them before it is your turn to be bitten. There is as much adventure at the corner of rue d'Ulm as among the dunes of the Sahara. The new frontier of microbiology. The foreign student of twenty-two, seated before a stack of newspapers, is still living off his mother. Like all males at the time, he wears a close-trimmed beard and dark jacket, eats in low dives where working men down their drink with the words 'That's another glass the Boche won't have!' Followed by: 'Look, landlord, we'd be fools to leave them the barrel!' Yersin himself writes: 'I witnessed a violent set-to between some workmen and a person of German origin, I think, who'd had the misfortune to speak his native language, he was beaten almost senseless.'

For the moment, it is he who is going through hard times. He enrols in the first bacteriology course given by Professor Cornil. It is a new discipline. His whole life long, Yersin is to choose the new, the 'absolutely modern'.

In Pasteur's consulting rooms, in the space of a few months, they perform as many inoculations as they can. In January 1886: of nearly a thousand patients vaccinated, six die – four after being bitten by wolves, two by dogs. In July: almost two thousand successes and no more than ten failures. The bodies are sent to the mortuary at Hôtel-Dieu Hospital, where Cornil tasks Yersin with performing autopsies on them. The verdict of the Carl Zeiss microscope is final: observation of the spinal cord proves that the vaccine failed to take effect. The patients were treated too late. Yersin hands the results to Pasteur's assistant, Émile Roux. It is the moment when the two orphans first meet, standing in their white coats in the Hôtel-Dieu mortuary, surrounded by the cadavers of rabies victims, and it is to change their lives.

The (paternal) orphan from Morges in French Switzerland and the orphan from Confolens in south-west France.

Roux introduces Yersin to Pasteur. The shy novice, having found the place, comes face to face with the man. He writes to Fanny: 'Mr Pasteur's practice is small, four-square, with two large windows. By one window is a small table with, set out on it, stemmed glasses containing the viruses to be used in inoculations.'

Before long Yersin is working with them at the rue d'Ulm practice. Each morning a long line of rabies victims forms in the courtyard. Pasteur auscultates, Roux and Grancher inoculate, Yersin assists. He is taken on, paid a meagre salary. Never again will he be in anyone's debt. In the austere scientist from the Jura, the orphan from Morges and the orphan from Confolens have found a father. The man in the black frockcoat with the grand biblical name, the 'shepherd of his sheep' who will guide flocks to pastures new and souls towards redemption.

At the Academy of Sciences, Louis Pasteur, a sick man, still administrator of the École Normale Supérieure, finishes his talk. There is justification for setting up an institution to inoculate against rabies. The City of Paris is placing at his disposal, on a provisional basis, a ramshackle three-floor brick-and-timber building in rue Vauquelin, where the Pasteurian crowd will take up residence. It is the start of their communal life. Around the courtyard, stables, kennels, the inoculation room. The team squat the rooms of the floors above. Roux, Loir, Grancher, Viala, Wasserzug, Mechnikov, Haffkine, Yersin. The latter will frown and take offence when people pronounce his name 'Yair-*seen*', like Haffkine, because of his accent. He leaves the house each morning to attend his medical lectures in rue des Saints-Pères. He lunches in a little bar in rue Gay-Lussac. For his thesis he chooses diphtheria and tuberculosis, which in poetry is still called 'consumption'. He conducts clinical observations at the Enfants-Malades children's hospital, takes samples from the backs of swollen throats, extracts membranes, tries to isolate the diphtheria toxin, reads explorers' accounts in periodicals.

An international subscription fund is opened at the Banque de France for Louis Pasteur. Money comes pouring in. The Tsar of Russia, the Emperor of Brazil and the Sultan of Istanbul all contribute, but so do humbler folk whose names are printed in the official government gazette each morning. Old Pasteur pores over the lists. He weeps on seeing that young Joseph Meister has sent three *sous*. A plot of land is acquired in the fifteenth arrondissement. Roux and Yersin go over to rue Dutot weekly to inspect the work, returning to rue d'Ulm to find the little crowd gathered in the Pasteurs' flat, with the plans spread out before them. The old man in the black frockcoat has already had two strokes, his speech is impaired, his left arm paralysed, and he walks with a limp. Roux and Yersin, working with the architect, design an internal staircase for the new Institute with smaller steps and more of them.

For old Pasteur, there are to be no more discoveries. He will be succeeded by Roux, the chosen one, the finest of his sons, the heir apparent. Pasteur's final battle is theoretical. For over twenty years his foes, the champions of spontaneous generation, have kept popping up almost miraculously. He remains adamant: nothing comes from nothing. But what of God? Why all these microbes, why keep them hidden all this time? Why the dead children, mostly from poor families? Fanny is concerned. Will Pasteur be like Darwin before him? The origin of species and biological evolution, from microbe to man, in defiance of Holy Writ. It makes Yersin smile, Yersin and the whole crowd. Soon all will be clear, one need only explain, instruct, repeat the experiments. How could they possibly have known that, a hundred and fifty years later, half the world's population would still argue for creationism?

During those years when the little Pasteurian crowd is coming together, the little crowd of Saharians continues to meet in rue Mazarine, while the little crowd of Parnassians evaporates. For a while, the three crowds cohabit. In the same city and in the same streets. The gentle poet Banville is still dossing in rue de Buci, where he lends his garret room to Rimbaud before the latter moves to rue Racine to live with Verlaine. Its clairvoyant gone, the Parnassian crowd slides into decline. It still, out of habit, frequents its labs, the neighbourhood bars, where very different elixirs grow in retorts. The rainbow sprites who take up residence in the heads of the now decrepit Parnassians go on watering the lurking alexandrine that ceaselessly replicates itself in diptychs, yet ones that grow ever more anaemic. In this age of the absolutely modern microscope and syringe, the alexandrine breathes its last, slain with a masterstroke by the young poet who has left to sell rifles to the Shoa king, Menelik II, future Emperor of Ethiopia.

Yersin for his part reads voraciously, but only works of science or accounts of explorations. He works in quietness and solitude, looking like an idler and with the air of one who simply does not care. That, for him, is style. At night, he boils up his microbe stews and prepares his reagents. He is mesmerised by the amount of material at his disposal. Practical work at last. Building kites. He opens the doors of chicken cages and mouse cages, takes samples, inoculates and then, by a stroke of genius, infects a rabbit with a new type of experimental tuberculosis: typho-bacillary, it is called, or typhobacillosis.

The slight young man in black takes it back to the lab and hands the test tube to Roux. Or rather draws the white rabbit out of the hat, holding it by its two ears and depositing it on the bench. Look what I've found. Roux adjusts the burred focusing wheel of the microscope between thumb and forefinger, looks up, turns and eyes the shy student with a frown. 'Yersin Tuberculosis' enters the textbooks of medical instruction, and that in itself ensures that his name passes into posterity for general practitioners and historians of medicine. But the wider public will soon have forgotten a name that, plague notwithstanding, is hardly common knowledge today. The poor sick rabbit coughs up its lungs and falls dead on the bench. Droplets of red blood stain the white fur. Its martyrdom earns the young man his first publication in the Institute's journal, the *Annales de l'Institut Pasteur* – an article signed by Roux and Yersin. Though the latter is not even a doctor at this point, nor even a Frenchman as yet.

Three years after arriving in Paris, Yersin, now twenty-five, writes his thesis, defends it and is awarded a bronze medal, which he slips into his pocket to give to Fanny. Next day he is pronounced doctor of medicine and boards the evening train for Germany. Pasteur has asked him to enrol in the technical microbiology course just launched by Robert Koch, discoverer of the tuberculosis bacillus, at Berlin's Institute of Hygiene. Yersin, being Swiss, is bilingual. Here we almost enter the world of espionage. The man whom Yersin's notebooks call 'the great lama Koch' attacks Pasteur vehemently in his writings. Yersin attends all twenty-four lectures, fills notebooks, translates Koch's words for Pasteur's benefit, sketches a laboratory plan, draws up a report and concludes that it should not be too difficult to do better in Paris.

On his return, a second publication signed Roux and Yersin comes out. The buildings of the Pasteur Institute are inaugurated with great pomp by head of state Sadi Carnot and his international guests. Yersin is still Swiss at this time, but the practice of medicine in France is reserved by law to citizens of the Republic. He takes steps accordingly, sending off a letter to Fanny. His maternal grandparents were French, so the problem is quickly solved. Protestants, fleeing religious persecution. France welcomes home her prodigal son.

Back in rue Vauquelin the two men, though not short of other things to do, hang up their white coats one afternoon and don jackets. Roux accompanies his assistant to the town hall of the fifth arrondissement in place du Panthéon. A stone's throw away. The two men sign the register. The clerk blots the certificate and hands it over. Not even taking time to celebrate with a drink, as Parnassians would have done, they return to the lab, resume their white coats, relight the Bunsen burners, and reach for the bacillus stew. Yersin is a French scientist.

rejection

But what if he had stayed Swiss? Or taken German citizenship? What if this old man, dozing in his aeroplane seat, white of beard and blue of eye, his spirit calm – what if he had chosen Koch over Pasteur? Where would he be today, at seventy-seven, if he held a Reich passport? People of genius frequently let themselves be abused. They are known for their naivety. Those who invent weapons of mass destruction purely for the pleasure of solving a problem would not hurt a fly. Suppose that, as this war broke out, Yersin were an elderly retired doctor, living in Berlin. If he had married a Marburg girl, where would his children and grandchildren be today, wearing which uniform?

The aircraft will be above the Rhône now, flying over

vineyards and green grapes under the sun of May '40. And the conscripts, will they be back for the harvest? There is a risk involved in taking a stance like Yersin, always trying to wash one's hands of politics. Turning one's back on History and its awful fruit. An individualist, as altruists often are. It is later in life, from loving others too much, that a person becomes a misanthrope.

Yersin, willy-nilly, always has to know everything. He opens his notebook, asks questions of the crew of the little white metal whale. The Air France hydroplane, this flying boat making for Marseilles, is a LeO, named after its two designers, Lioré and Olivier, a LeO H-242. Its fuselage is of anodised Duralumin. He notes that down. It is a new material, anodised Duralumin. He wonders what new thing he might build in Asia, using anodised Duralumin. The eleven passengers around him sit in comfy, high-backed seats. Drinks are 'on the house'.

Surrounded by so many rich refugees, cowardly plutocrats who will select at random, depending on where they land, a holiday spot in which to hide out with their loot, Yersin shields his privacy with the notebooks, feigning concentration. His name and face are familiar. He is the last survivor of the Pasteur crowd. He is known to be going as far as Saigon, the last stop, an eight-day journey. By steamer it takes a month. But each sea trip enables him to bring back crate-fuls of equipment, glassware for the experiments, seeds for his fields. War will interrupt communications once again. It was the same shambles after '14.

Fifty years have passed since Yersin opted to leave Europe. Asia was where he spent the First World War and will be spending the Second. Alone. The way he has always lived. Or rather, surrounded by his little crowd in the fishing village of Nha Trang. Yersin's crowd. Because with the passing years the loner has emerged as a leader of men. Out there he has created something approaching a community, a lay monastery that lives apart from the world and that he will now be rejoining. As if under vows of frugality and celibacy as well as of fraternity, his scientific and agricultural community of Nha Trang is not unlike an anarchist Cecilia, as it was called, or Fourieristic phalanstery, with him as white-bearded patriarch. Yersin will simply shrug whenever the idea is mentioned to his face. The fact is, somewhat by chance, without having truly wished it, preoccupied by something quite different, he now controls a substantial fortune.

Once only, in a bid for assimilation, to regularise his position and conform to Faculty tradition, did Alexandre Yersin, as a very young doctor, a very young Frenchman, a very young researcher, decide he should also be a very young husband. Louis Pasteur was married, after all, and it never prevented him from working. Yersin enjoyed dining at the couple's small flat in rue d'Ulm. The two men got on well, stern, upright, taciturn individuals with eyes as blue as snow and ice. He too would become a wise old man enjoying the tender affections of an aged spouse.

In fact, he did something about it, applying the same rational methods as he had used to attest his genealogy. As ever, a missive to his mother. A letter to Fanny.

Having traced his ancestry for him, she now, on the instant, finds him a fiancée. Mina Schwarzenbach. The niece of a friend. Pretty, Mina is. A virgin, presumably, buttoned all the way up to her lace collar, though perhaps, of an evening, beneath the long black skirt, a middle finger will stir the fire. Yersin sets about writing to her. It is hard work, far tougher than a piece on diphtheria. Several drafts finish up in the wastepaper basket. Dear Mina. He may have sung the praises of the peaceful old Pasteur couple. The learned discussions held around their table with archaeologist Perrot, director of the École Normale Supérieure, and the account of his expeditions in Asia Minor. That is clumsy. Mina Schwarzenbach wants to read impassioned alexandrines dedicated to her alone. Come evening, holding the letter in her other hand, she will reread them. Yersin is behaving like an ass. He is sent packing. He draws a veil over the episode. Having a wife on his coat tails would soon have got in the way, he realises. Or: we'll see about that later, when I've been round the world, really considered the matter.

For now, I should really like to see the sea.

Normandy

To Roux the idea seems utterly crazy. See the sea. He turns off his Bunsen burner, wipes his hands on his lab coat, throws up his arms. He must be dreaming. See the sea. Why not end one's days in a fishing village? Well, actually, says Yersin ... But enough said. Look, he's had an idea. How to turn the useful into the pleasurable. Playing on his minor notoriety as a tuberculosis expert, young Dr Yersin has persuaded the Schools Inspectorate to send him on a mission to Grandcamp in the Calvados department. He is going to examine the bugs in the mouths of children living in a healthy location and breathing plenty of fresh air. These he will then compare with the ones found in the mouths of

Parisian schoolchildren. Find out whether perhaps having the sky polluted by factory smoke is an aggravating factor in disease. He has just purchased one of the new bicycles with a chain and cogwheels, manufactured by Armand Peugeot.

Yersin packs his suitcase, wraps up his microscope, takes the Dieppe train, rides to Le Havre by bicycle, boards the ferry to Honfleur and pedals as far as Grandcamp. In the mornings he tours classrooms, where children step up to him and open their mouths wide; the evenings he spends strolling along the waterfront, chatting to fishermen, who agree to take him out some time. At night, in the inn, he reads Pierre Loti's *An Iceland Fisherman*. He and Loti have in common that they had been loners since childhood. Both were born into upright families of modest means and brought up in the provinces under strict Protestantism, with no father at home. They grew up among women, harbouring a latent misogyny, an ambiguous sexuality and a dream of sailing the seas and oceans of the world. Except that the idea comes to one sooner in Rochefort-sur-mer, in a sailor family, than in Vaudois Morges.

Yersin, twenty-six, is seeing the sea for the first time.

Not from high on a cliff top with windblown hair like a Parnassian poet but from the deck of the trawler *Raoul*, buffeted by rough seas, wearing boots and oilskins, perhaps helping to raise sails and lower them, knowing the satisfaction of a job well done.

In his enthusiasm, and for the benefit of Fanny, his sole reader, he pens an imitation of Loti or of those explorers who first came upon exotic peoples. His pastiche evokes a world of men, a band-of-brothers world, somewhere between Loti and Victor Hugo's *Toilers of the Sea*, even though Yersin knows nothing as yet of ships' superstructures or the fact that no one, on board ship, ever says 'rope' – any more than one would in the house of a hanged man:

Abruptly, the boat came to a halt, the rope holding the net stretched to breaking point. 'Quick, furl the sails, we've struck a large rock that has torn the net badly, so be quick, bring needles and twine to mend the holes.' It was nigh on seven in the evening before the net was once more usable, but turbot is a daytime catch. At night, they fish sole – also much sought-after, but it involves hugging the shore: sole prefer a sandy sea bottom, clear of stones.

In the evening they grill red mullet on board. Then everyone except two men on watch and the passenger 'goes to bed in his berth'. Fanny, perusing such missives in the little chintz parlour of Fig Tree House, feels a touch disappointed. Some bits ring false.

Like a good paternal orphan, Yersin meets all his mother's wishes. He becomes a doctor. My son is a doctor, mothers will say. This one was more. A scientist. He works with

Pasteur, his 'right-hand man', she says. But that will do. She wants him back in Morges with her. Let him bask in his glory, open consulting rooms on the shore of the Lake, sport his brass plate. Fanny worries. Mothers always worry. He may have a weak blood vessel in his head. Like his father, and we know what happened there. He is insatiable, this son. What will he think of next? He has this idea of living among savages. As if the French were not bad enough. She rereads the letter that has just arrived: 'I shall be glad to leave Paris, the theatre bores me, I can't abide society, and it is no way to live, not keeping on the move.'

After Normandy, he has it all planned. Neat as a seaman's knot. Yersin has no intention of spending the rest of his life surrounded by test tubes. Eye glued to the microscope rather than sweeping the horizon. Sea air is what he needs. Silence and solitude. Yet here is Roux, who clearly knows more about bugs than men, thinking he is doing him an honour by, on Yersin's return from Normandy, putting him in charge of the microbiology course.

For Yersin, skilled in the Socratic method, nothing that can be taught is worth learning, even if all ignorance is reprehensible. He is a brilliant autodidact, always will be, feeling nothing but contempt for sloggers. All one needs is the ability to observe. Lacking that, one will never learn anything. Between the orphan from Confolens and the orphan from

Morges, mutual incomprehension spirals. 'It led to a slanging match that went on for two hours or more.'

The former pontificates to the latter, reminding him of his duty as a Pasteurian. But for God's sake, Yersin, thousands would sell their sisters to be in your shoes, while you … Words fail him in the presence of this shy young man on the threshold of a splendid future. That hard blue gaze. It takes his breath away. To Yersin, scientific research is like playing the violin. A brilliant dabbler, touched by grace. Absolute pitch or, in this case, absolute vision, coupled with the good fortune without which talent is nothing. Mozart opting to become a woodcutter. Rimbaud flogging Mocha coffee or rifles from Liège. And now here was Yersin, boring him with an account of his bicycle ride and fishing trips on a trawler. Roux thinks he may have drawn the wrong horse. Perhaps Yersin is a comet: and at twenty-six, as occasionally happens with mathematicians and poets, the light has already gone out.

the tall iron tower at the
centre of the world

Nevertheless, the course is a success. Yersin speaks the few essential words. The rest presupposes an ability to observe. A lab assistant, rather in the manner of a conjuror or head waiter, sets the zinc tray down before each attendee and removes the glass cover. Wearing gloves, the student then grasps some dead rodent that has succumbed to one of the diseases in the prospectus. Syringes plunge into fur. Drops of polluted blood are smeared on slides and placed under the microscope.

Roux having delivered the first two microbiology lectures, Yersin is in charge of the next two. The announcement has been circulating for months in the medical press and in newspapers the world over. This is the new age of the undersea cable. Doctors climb the gangplanks of steamboats, disembarking at the transatlantic ports of Bordeaux, St Nazaire and Cherbourg. At the harbour station they board the Paris train. This summer's lecture course coincides with the Universal Exhibition and the centenary of the French Revolution, the zenith of the Age of Enlightenment.

Paris is becoming the international capital of medicine, and at its heart the brand-new red bricks of the Pasteur Institute shine as a beacon of Progress. Everything about the Institute is new, the gleaming floors and the shiny ceramic work surfaces. Stone window surrounds and Louis XIII façade. The idea is already emerging of setting up Pasteur Institutes abroad and launching programmes of preventive and curative vaccination. Assembled in front of Yersin in the large room lit by tall, small-paned windows are not just hospital doctors from all corners of France but also a Belgian, a Swede, a Cuban, three Russians, three Mexicans, a Dutchman, three Italians, a Britisher, a Romanian, an Egyptian and an American. Twelve nationalities, if the arithmetic is right, but not a single German. Bad sign, that.

Some days, in the gravel-strewn courtyard with its young chestnut trees, the aged hemiplegic in the black frockcoat and bow tie, a living legend already, can be seen sitting on a bench in the sun. People try to have themselves photographed with him. The picture will look good in the waiting room, up there with the Pasteur Institute certificate. Yersin finds this tiresome. 'It is a big irritation and takes up masses of time. At my first class we had Mr Pasteur, Mr Chamberland and a host of other intimidating figures. Mr Pasteur seemed satisfied.'

After the lecture, the young man goes for a stroll alone, along the Seine embankment. Black of beard and blue of eye. His third publication, on diphtheria, came out that spring. Yersin's genius is not on the wane, the light has not gone out. As the first denizen of the Institute, he chose the finest corner room, very light, he likes comfort whenever possible. He introduces incubators and autoclaves, takes deliveries of glassware.

That summer the statue of Danton is erected at carrefour de l'Odéon to mark the centenary of the Revolution. In the Champ de Mars and all along quai d'Orsay there are displays not simply of scientific and technological progress but of French civilisation, in effect, as it spreads the wide white wings of its genius to the ends of the earth. On the open ground in front of Les Invalides, the War and Colonial ministries have paid for reproductions of Senegalese, Tahitian, Tunisian and Cambodian villages, importing whole populations in order to evoke these remote lands on the fringes of the French Empire. Everything sets out to be universalist while evincing a deep-rooted nationalism. For a Swiss, this has always been the paradox of French universalism, starting with their Declaration: the ideology of the Republic, forever seeming so odd to other nations in that, even in its self-utterance, it reveals a quality less universalist than it claims.

Opening his notebook in the Gallery of Machines, Yersin finds all he sees quite as captivating as medicine: mining and metallurgy, machine tools, mineral-water bottling plant, civil engineering and public works. This is what he thinks of as study. Only one thing is required: observation. And Yersin does plenty of that. Later, he will busy himself with machines as he did with kites, taking them apart, reassembling them, making improvements – always a far sounder method than reading the instructions. This is a time of resolute optimism. Gustave Eiffel and Jules Verne. An early novel of Verne's, *Paris in the Twentieth Century*, is in fact a denunciation of Progress, a book of apocalyptic anticipation set in an age when art and literature have been broken and brought low by science and technology. A complete turkey. Be more positive, is the advice of his shrewd editor Hetzel. Black Romanticism is old hat. Eulogise science and the machine. Jules Ferry. State education. The Cartesian fable. Then the centennial Fourteenth of July arrives. A century after storming the Bastille and lighting up the Paris sky by setting fire to the stores of powder, the French, grown wiser, take the lift to the top of the tall iron tower, gaze out over the city as they inaugurate its new landmark, applaud a peaceful firework display.

The world's doctors return to their foreign landscapes, their pampas and their taigas, each with a tiny bronze Eiffel Tower and a signed photograph of Pasteur, possibly a garter too as a maudlin souvenir of the Moulin Rouge or the Folies Bergères. Yersin shuts his notebook. 'Yesterday I finished my course with a deep sigh of contentment. The students can come back and tidy up their bits and pieces, then the lab will be quiet again.' Pasteur makes sure his young minion receives the appropriate academic decoration. Indifferent to the bauble, Yersin slips it into his pocket to give to Fanny.

There will not be Koch Institutes all over the world, Berlin will have no tall iron tower and no Universal Exhibition. Bismarck is mired in his African problems. The pressure keeps mounting beneath spike-topped helmets that lack a safety valve. In a country where Prussians are wondering if it was worth winning the war and capturing, at Sedan, the imperial head of this bothersome neighbour. Because between Paris and Berlin, and in some sense between Pasteur and Koch, lies Sedan.

Returning to Morges in late summer, Yersin is a local hero, less for his work on tuberculosis and diphtheria (not subjects one discusses at table, as Fanny tells her charges) than for having been present at the two Parisian inaugurations most talked about in French-speaking Switzerland, that of the Pasteur Institute and that of the World Fair. Fanny invites the gossip columnists to Fig Tree House on the shore of the Lake. They drink tea in the little chintz parlour with, on the wall, the bronze medal and the academic decorations. She takes advantage of the occasion to organise a deportment lesson and a small-talk drill for the young bags. Yersin talks about the world villages, the machines, the four hanging restaurants, one in each pillar with its riveted cross-braces, and about how, for five francs, he rode up to the third level of the tall iron tower. And the fashions? Has he brought back brochures? Yersin puts his cup and saucer down on the embroidered table-mat and says in soft, enigmatic tones:

'Most importantly, I saw the sea.'

Fanny shrugs.

The sea.

ship's doctor

Pasteur and Roux have to bow to the evidence. They are not going to tie Yersin down. Better to find an amicable solution, keep the hothead researcher on the organisation's books while allowing him his freedom. Give youth time to pass. Then one day, like Odysseus ... Reluctantly, Pasteur dictates a reference:

I, the undersigned, director of the Pasteur Institute, member of the French Institute, holder of the Grand Cross of the Legion of Honour, do certify that Dr Yersin (Alexandre) has worked as laboratory assistant at the Physiological Chemistry Laboratory of the College of Higher Education and subsequently at the Pasteur Institute from July 1886 to the present. I am happy to say that Dr Yersin consistently performed his functions most assiduously and that, while at my laboratory, he published several studies that were well received by competent scientists.

The letter, addressed to the head office of the shipping firm Messageries Maritimes in Bordeaux, is enclosed with Yersin's application for a job as ship's doctor.

The company's reply is warm and spontaneous, and the applicant is asked, should it become necessary to organise a change of medical personnel, to choose what part of the world would suit him. Yersin chooses Asia. In recruiting him, the company places great reliance on a certain commercial consideration:

'And do you know, my dear, I was examined during the voyage by one of those young Pasteurians, and we talked about dear old Pasteur ... '

For the next few weeks Yersin once again does the rounds of the capital's hospitals to prepare himself, leaving nothing to chance, and acquire skills he has previously neglected – skin disorders, minor surgery, ophthalmology. He buys a set of instruments suitable for general practice and a wicker cabin trunk into which he crams his books, the Carl Zeiss microscope, a pair of navy binoculars and a complete photographic kit including trays, enlarger and bottles of developer and fixative. He boards the train for Marseilles, where ancient parapets line the quays.

The microbiology course is entrusted to Haffkine, hitherto the Institute's librarian, a Ukrainian Jew, another orphan adopted by the Pasteurian crowd. We shall come across him again in Bombay, Haffkine, at the centre of one of those controversies of which the scientific world is so fond. Yersin takes his seat in the carriage. He has spent a total of five years in Paris. He will return there from time to time, but never again will he live in the city.

Marseilles

The airspace is not safe on this last day of May '40. Earlier in the afternoon, much faster Stukas, flying higher than the little white whale, gathered in a show of nosediving, sirens screaming, before circling back over the Mediterranean to return to base. Four years later, towards the end of the war, Saint-Exupéry will disappear at the controls of his Lightning. He is another Lutetia regular, the last survivor of the Mermoz crowd.

The little white whale describes an arc before touching down on Étang de Berre. Its floats carve furrows in the surface of the lagoon, raising a spray of glittering foam. The swaying cabin finds its equilibrium. They reach the pontoon.

The news is not good. In Paris, the airport has closed. The Luftwaffe is shelling roads and bridges. The crew are worried. There is talk of stalags. Some members will desert at the end of the line, the bravest becoming fighter pilots and joining the squadrons assembling in Algiers or Brazzaville. After filling up, the plane takes off for Corfu, next stop on the Asia route. The little white whale overflies the port of Marseilles at sunset. Looking down, Yersin sees ships tied at their berths like long fish. Fifty years earlier, almost to the day, he walked along one of those quays, prior to embarking on the *Oxus*.

None can have imagined, back in 1890, the eruption, twenty-four years later, of a conflict that will be called the Great War, then soon afterwards the World War, and now, since a few days back, the First World War. Nor can anyone have conceived the swift advance of aviation. An amazing invention, making it possible to reduce distances and drop bombs on whole populations. Before '14, Yersin had considered buying a plane. He paid a special visit to the aerodrome at Chartres to make his first flight and discuss prices, envisaged laying out a landing strip at Nha Trang, but in the end abandoned the idea, turning to something else. Typical Yersin. Jumping from one thing to another. He'll not be a sailor for long.

While Clément Ader is coaxing the world's first powered aircraft off the ground and the very word *avion* is passing into the French language, at Marseilles' St Charles station Yersin is alighting from the train that has brought him from Paris. He is twenty-seven. Walking down the Canebière to the Old Port, he is seeing the sea for the second time. The water is bluer than off Dieppe, the waves more languid. He enters the port of Marseilles, and it's quite something, this gateway to the world. Fifteen years back, Conrad began his sailing career here. Ten years back, Rimbaud embarked for the Red Sea and Arabia. Brazza re-embarked for the Congo several months ago. A porter at Yersin's side pushes a hand truck bearing the wicker cabin trunk crammed with books, the bag of instruments, the microscope, the navy binoculars and the photographic equipment. Yersin climbs aboard the *Oxus*, bound for the Far East. He is handed a textbook entitled *Ship's Regulations*.

On every Messageries Maritimes liner the diurnal medical consultation is announced by a bell. The doctor takes orders from the captain only, at whose table he eats. He is in charge of the ship's pharmacy, which he stocks up at each port of call. He is also responsible for checking the cleanliness of the galleys and the freshness of supplies. A male nurse greets Yersin, throwing open the door of his first-class cabin, all brass and polished wood, and handing him his white uniform with the five gold stripes. Yersin adjusts its folds before a mirror. He loves order and luxury. Because luxury means calm. The worst thing about poverty, which he loathes, is constantly being importuned. Never being able to keep oneself to oneself.

The ship takes on several hundred passengers, this time including, in the bowels of the vessel, a troop of soldiers making for their garrison in Tonkin, which has been a French protectorate for the last seven years. In second-class accommodation, groups of Benedictine monks and Sisters of Charity whom God has called to China. Plus, with one-way tickets, the usual crowd of villains, con men, bankrupts, pimps and sons of good family, off to see whether life is any more tolerable in the colonies.

Back on the quay, Yersin shades his eyes with one hand and sizes up the brute against the light. Rather different from a Normandy trawler. A towering wall of steel held fast to the wharf by hawsers, one hundred and twenty-five metres from end to end. The stokers have fired up the boilers, the pressure is building. The officers, ashore for one last evening, lounge on sunlit café terraces. Strolling alone along the docks, a striking young man wearing a white uniform with five gold stripes fills his lungs with the air of the open sea, the air of adventure, a rich milord that some creature of the night no doubt invites into her crib to explore other horizons. Did Mina Schwarzenbach, he wonders, see all this coming?

at sea

White handkerchiefs flutter – waved, perhaps, by wives left behind with swarms of kids. The sounds of a brass band and the singing of a choir to bid the missionaries Godspeed. The huge liner, dressed from bow to stern with multicoloured flags, slips her moorings and swings out into the roads. And for the first time Yersin knows what sailors mean by the words.

They are at sea by late afternoon. Notre Dame de la Garde has shrunk to invisibility beyond their wake. The evening light paints the hull pink and tinges the plumage of their seagull escort with yellow. The wind strengthens, whipping up the waves. The passengers make for the saloons.

Mah-jong in first, belote in steerage. It is a thirty-day voyage from Marseilles to Saigon.

First stop Messina, followed by Crete. That far is little more than rock-dodging, but eventually, turning south, they head straight across the Mediterranean for Alexandria, where seven years earlier the young Pasteurian Thuillier died while studying the cholera epidemic. Yersin arranges a little study corner in his cabin, filling the shelves of polished wood with medical textbooks and his English dictionary. On the desk below, he opens his notebooks, writes his letters to Fanny. One morning, up on the bridge, he sees the ship approaching pale sandy beaches and skinny palms, soon distinguishes his first minaret, then his first camel: like Flaubert, on catching his first glimpse of Egypt he takes in 'a bellyful of colours as a donkey will stuff itself with oats'.

The *Oxus* enters the set of locks. As Yersin sails into the Suez Canal in that spring of 1890, the British explorer Henry Stanley, hero of the Congress of Berlin five years earlier, the man who found Livingstone, who crossed Africa from coast to coast, is closeted in a villa in Cairo, writing an account of his Equatoria expedition in search of Emin Pasha and his return via Zanzibar. He calls it *In Darkest Africa*.

Thousands of kilometres farther south, Brazza and Conrad, each aboard a riverboat, are steaming up the Congo. The British captain, who was a Pole before adopting Marseilles, set his novella *Heart of Darkness* in the northernmost reaches of the river, at Stanley Falls. From that same city of Cairo, three years back, Arthur Rimbaud, the renegade of the Parnassian crowd, currently holed up with his servant Djami Wadai in a room at the Hôtel Europe, was still writing to his sister that Egypt would be only a stopover. 'I might go on to Zanzibar, from where one can make long forays into Africa, and possibly on to China, Japan, who knows where?'

Leaving the monotonous banks of the canal, the ship drives on through the smooth, translucent waters of the Red Sea. The abrupt discovery of fearsome heat, metal rendered too hot to touch by the bright white sun, the purple mountains of Yemen, wafts of evening breeze as the vessel draws near to Aden. At night, people come out on deck to seek coolness in the still air beneath stars that have an unfamiliar sparkle. Yersin's notebook brims with sentences that pre-echo Lowry's *Ultramarine*: 'We see large dark masses peeling away from the shore, faintly lit by the red flames of many torches, and from these rafts towed by small steam lauches there arises a rhythmic chanting formed of several notes. Colliers are coming out to refill the bunkers of the *Oxus*.' He finishes his letter to Fanny: 'How far one already feels from Europe!'

The squaddies have slipped into their colonial shorts and donned sun hats. Each morning, on deck, they perform their gymnastics and weapons drill. After three days the ship leaves on the longest stage of the trip, hauling anchor for the slow descent of the Indian Ocean. Course is set south-east for Colombo. Water tanks and coal bunkers have been recharged, the holds are packed with everything not yet produced in Saigon – machine tools, firearms, evening gowns, hectolitres of plonk and pastis, appliances to make ice cubes. With the weight of all this clobber beneath the black splendour of its single funnel, the vessel bears down on the green waves with its three thousand eight hundred tonnes, there is the occasional short stinging rainshower, then out comes the sun again, making the streaming woodwork gleam.

They enter the tropics, spotting the odd untouched island in the middle of nowhere with its quiff of coconut palms, and they are back in Baudelaire's day, when the alexandrine still sparkled. A sleepy island where nature provides curious trees bearing luscious fruit. Yersin is becoming familiar with his surroundings and his function, the hundreds of metres of deck and the kilometre or more of gangways and companionways, the rhythm of the brass bell that rings for early-afternoon surgery. An elegant, white-uniformed Barnabooth who, each morning, listens while the officers of the watch give their report in the captain's wardroom.

In the evenings, he resumes his medical reading or studies English. The few Brits he encounters in the first-class saloon will be disembarking in India or in Singapore, returning to their plantations in Malaya or Siam. He learns of the British habit of forming adjectives from acronyms. That year, on the liners, the word 'posh' is coined, from the initial letters of 'port out, starboard home', because it is deemed the height of fashion to attune one's reservation to the direction of the ship. One can thus, on both legs of the trip, enjoy from one's cabin a view of the changing coastline, while the rest, who are not 'posh' and lack proper foresight, see only ocean.

While strolling back and forth between the saloon and his cabin, Yersin sails into the South Seas. He sees tropical rain-forest in Ceylon, warm rain falling on broad emerald-green leaves. In the saloon, as the vessel crosses to Singapore, the old colonials, absinthe in hand, tell him the story of Mayréna, who was once King Marie I. This former cavalryman of the French Expeditionary Corps turned adventurer and jungle explorer carved out a kingdom for himself of which no one knew the exact location, somewhere in Annam, declaring himself King of the Sedang before being driven out by the French. People say he is now living in retirement near by, on Tioman Island, surrounded by his now-deposed court of henchmen turned barons and the troupe of faded dancers attired in pink frills and furbelows who had come out from Brussels at the height of his grandeur.

After Singapore the ship sails around the Gulf of Siam off Bangkok and turns north-east past the Mekong delta before reaching, farther north, Cap St Jacques.

*

The tall, steep-sided liner enters Saigon River at high tide and steams inland beneath another low and heavy sky, its speed no more than two or three knots, walking pace, lest it upset the junks and sampans or bring down the shacks on stilts or disturb the fisheries built among mangroves. A gunboat precedes the vessel. The curious, anxious immigrants, elbows on rails, watch in their sticky clothing as cormorants dive into the reed-studded brown murk. Will they finally strike lucky here, they wonder, or are they doomed to end their days rotting away, surrounded by flooded rice paddies? Possibly one of them, more literate than the others (has he read Voltaire?), after embarking for the colonies as one might join the Foreign Legion, having been thwarted in love or failed at university, wonders: why *Oxus*, why name the ship after a river in central Asia that Genghis Khan caused to run red with Persian blood and filled with severed heads?

'Gradually the palm trees become taller, then one spots coconut groves where monkeys play. Eventually, after long stretches of open grassland, European-looking buildings come into view. The *Oxus* fires its cannon, drops anchor: we're here.' In the distance, warehouses, stocks of coal and cotton beneath tarpaulins, rows of barrels. On the quayside, swarms of rickshaws and victorias hitched up to small Annamite horses. Columns of squaddies go marching off two by two, heading for temporary barracks before moving on to Tonkin, right up north on the Chinese border. The priests and nuns take the other direction, rue Catinat, which runs straight up from the river to the plateau and to the place Francis-Garnier, where the two new bell towers of Notre Dame Cathedral stand as well as the recently built central post office, the Poste de Gustave Eiffel.

Seated on bales to one side, their pockets stuffed with packs of cards and knives, the pimps eye the stragglers, the passengers no one has come to meet, the fresh arrivals from Marseilles like that year's partridges, ripe for plucking in the brothels and opium dens of Saigon's Chinatown. Yersin, accompanied by the ship's officers, visits the Arsenal before relaxing on the terrace of the Rex or the Majestic. White-suited businessmen sip vermouth and glasses of blackcurrant liqueur of an evening. The city of Saigon is less than thirty years old. Its buildings are white, its streets broad, traced on the Haussmann model, shaded by carobs. At the shipping line's agency, the young medic has his papers returned with a fresh sprinkling of the stamps of the maritime customs and the health services: Dr Yersin is to embark on the *Volga* in four days' time.

The *Volga* serves the Saigon–Manila line.

parallel lives

The *Volga* is an ancient vessel powered by both sail and steam, rigged as a three-masted schooner, one boiler amidships, a smallish vessel for sixty-seven passengers and several metric tons of cargo.

Each month, on the outward voyage from Saigon, the line's regular merchants ship European products destined for wealthy inhabitants of the Philippines: garments from Paris and porcelain from Limoges, crystal decanters and fine wines. For the return trip, they bring in exchange, in the bowels of the ship, products of the sweat of the Filipino poor: sugar loaves, Manila cigars, cocoa nibs. From port to port, it is three days' and three nights' voyage on Conrad's

South China Sea with its deep, lazy swell that the bow pushes before it as if in a permanent sulk. The peaceable vessel advances with the aplomb of a ferry. Up on the bridge, Captain François Nègre is an old hand of the seaways of the Far East. For the next whole year, Yersin's life assumes the regularity of a pendulum.

He spends one third of it at sea, another third on shore leave in new Saigon, and the last third in old Manila. Like so many cities built by the Spanish, rich with centuries of history and a flamboyant Catholicism expressed in pure gold, statues of bleeding saints, votive plaques, garish virgins covered with offerings of flowers and fruit and cakes. All as strange, in the eyes of a Vaudois Puritan, as voodoo fetishes would seem. Overlooking the sea, a fortified citadel resembling those of Puerto Rico's San Juan or Havana in Cuba, steep paved streets leading up to a white cathedral fronted by twin bell towers, already gnawed by black rot and green moss at a time when the French have barely finished building their Notre Dame Cathedral in Saigon, using new red bricks from Toulouse.

But exploring those two cities takes him no time at all, and on each shore leave he ventures farther. He is an organised fellow, young Yersin, we know that. In the Philippines, he returns month after month to study astronomy with the

Jesuit fathers at the Observatory, he learns how to use a barometer to measure altitude, climbs the volcano named Taal and devotes himself to practical work as one might construct kites. He makes a pen-and-ink sketch of the volcano's crater. 'Down at the bottom are two yellowish green lagoons that give off clouds of dense white vapour. Here and there, small columns of smoke spout from crevasses.' He buys one of those boats that are here known as *bancas*, hires a pilot, sails up creeks, witnesses cockfights in Tagalog villages.

And each month Lord Jim/Yersin pushes farther up 'a narrow, twisting arroyo flowing through thick tropical jungle'. It is for Fanny, his sole reader, that he pens his first texts as an explorer. 'We advance beneath a vault of greenery, and you have to imagine, in addition, the moonlight, the nocturnal silence, and the fishermen's little canoes tucked away in dark bends of the creek, lending a peculiar charm to the scene. We pick up the major, his two dolls, and a Spanish sergeant. At one in the morning we reach Jala-Jala.' They turn back at dawn. Next day, using the cargo boom, the *banca* is hauled aboard the mother ship and stowed on deck. Weighing anchor, the *Volga* steams away. Yersin dons his white uniform with the five gold stripes and rings the bell. Later, in the wardroom, he continues the story of his excursions for the benefit of Captain Nègre and the merchants over their evening absinthe. The steamer resumes its slow rolling over the oily sea. Occasionally, sail is set, either to save coal or to honour the memory of the old days. The frail craft up on deck is the only thing linking Yersin's two lives. Three days later, back in Saigon, down it is lowered again into the water.

In Cochinchina, the Philippine *banca* becomes a Vietnamese sampan. Here, too, Yersin spends his time sailing up and down rivers. His two guides, Chun and Tiu, load blankets and lanterns, mosquito nets and the Chamberland filter, rice and live ducks with their legs trussed. 'The mountains, distant at first, draw closer, the creek narrows. The sun is tremendously hot at the bottom of this ravine.' As evening approaches, they pitch camp on the bank, light a fire, throttle and pluck the fowl. Soon the little troop are going up as far as Bien Hoa and beyond. There Yersin finds an isolated Danish planter, Jorgensen, and adopts the habit of accepting the old bear's hospitality. When Yersin leaves again, the man gives him a shopping list of things he expects to see in a month's time. The terrace of the teak house built on stilts overlooks the green expanse of the pepper plantation, and 'one sees beneath one's feet the water swirling amid rocks'. Away on the horizon, in the morning light, the mountains look blue. Elephants come down to the river to drink. The cries of monkeys and the raucous din of birdsong. This is where a man should live, apart from the world. With Jorgensen, he makes a two-day expedition to the nearest Moi villages.

In his letters, which an anxious Fanny begins hiding from the eyes of her girls at Fig Tree House, Yersin records his first ethnological observations, noting that the Moi 'are tall people, dressed very simply in a waistband. Facially, they differ strongly from Annamites. They are often bearded and moustached and have a haughtier, wilder look. Their villages consist of a single enormous house raised on stilts. Each family inhabits a compartment with rudimentary partitions. This is truly communal existence. Money is worth nothing for the Moi. They would rather have a few glass beads or a brass ring.'

Yersin feels the fascination of the inveterate loner for a life lived in common, the egalitarianism of primitive communism and the absence of money value. This is the way one should keep pushing forward, leave the water, yomp through forests, scale the Annamite Cordillera – cross it, even. Advance well beyond it, towards the country of the Sedang or the Jarai, where no one, not even Jorgensen, has ventured before. That Mayréna, maybe, who become King Marie I, but he was after gold or fame. Often Yersin goes back down to Saigon only the night before the *Volga* sails, re-embarking on his sampan, which three days later becomes his *banca* once more. Briefly, he rejoins Captain Nègre and the merchants. As for the crew, they are 'somewhat cosmopolitan, you'll find Chinese there, Malays, Cochinchinese'. He cannot imagine spending his whole life at sea like them, but he does not really know what else he can do. Before long he has reached the geographical limits of such peregrinations. It could all become as boring as a lecture course in microbiology.

Yersin is not yet an explorer, he has never gone straight on without turning back, never faced danger, never risked his life. Soon, in the fight with Thouk, a spear will pass through his body. His medical skills will save his life.

That same year, while Yersin is shuttling back and forth across the South China Sea between Manila and Saigon, the spring sees Rimbaud's final return to the port of Marseilles. After weeks of being stretchered across rocky ground with no nursing care and no Pasteurian products, the surgeon's saw takes off a leg. On board ship, the white-uniformed Messageries Maritimes doctor sits at his bedside, powerless. The delirious last words: the grand scansion of elephant tusks as jungle drums. Before the amputation the poet wrote to his sister, Isabelle: 'Why, at school, are we not taught what little medicine we should need to stop us doing such daft things?'

Albert & Alexandre

Calmette's arrival in Saigon takes Yersin by surprise. The two are meeting for the first time. It was Roux, back in Paris, acting on the advice of Pasteur, who arranged to bring them together.

Both men were born in the same year, but subsequently traced opposite trajectories. After studying medicine at the School of Naval Hygiene in Brest, Albert Calmette followed Admiral Courbet's China campaign, in which Pierre Loti also took part. A navy doctor, he was stationed in Hong Kong for a while, then did six months in Gabon, meeting Brazza there, followed by two years in Newfoundland, and was then posted to the St Pierre and Miquelon Islands. He recently completed the microbiology course at the Pasteur Institute, which sent him out to Cochinchina. Calmette is a new boy in the Pasteurian crowd.

Yersin has accepted the invitation out of politeness and curiosity. All that stuff belongs to his former life. Like a staging episode between navigation and research. When Calmette entered the navy's health service at the age of twenty, Yersin was in Marburg, never having seen the sea. Now he is the sailor, medical officer on the *Volga* for the past year. The two men sit down in a lounge of the Majestic, the white palace at the bottom of rue Catinat. Today's Dong Khoi.

Empire armchairs with gold trim, liveried pageboys. Looking out over the river full of junks, the same view as today, in 2012, more than one hundred and twenty years on. Let's choose a chair for the invisible ghost of the future. The writer with the moleskin notebook whom we met tracing Yersin's past from the Hotel Zur Sonne in Marburg. Now cocking an ear for, listening in to and recording the conversation of two twenty-eight-year-olds sporting neatly trimmed black beards. With the stealth of timid conspirators, the pair speak of their shared taste for geography, Loti and codfishing. In sweltering Saigon, they conjure up the snow and ice of Miquelon. The military man is the one in civvies, while the civilian wears the white uniform with the five gold stripes.

The towering shadow of the Commander of the Legion of Honour hovers over the young doctors, the tall, stern silhouette in the frockcoat and bow tie, his brow knitted, making its presence felt wherever and whenever two Pasteurians converse. Each will remember the day he first met the Old Man and have a story to tell. All will be familiar with the work and life of the man who, while never becoming a doctor, radically changed the course of medical history. The chemist and crystallographer. They will run through the stages of his success from the sickness of the silkworm butterfly, the fermentation of beer, the pasteurisation of wine and milk, the discovery of the bacilli behind swine erysipelas and anthrax in sheep, right up to the first inoculation against rabies. The inventor of a reality so deeply unsuspected in all the world's languages that he had to turn to Littré, disturbing him in the great work of compiling his dictionary. Littré had handed down a verdict, ruling that '*microbe* and *microbie* are perfectly good words. To denote animalcules, I should prefer *microbes*, firstly because, as you say, it is short, secondly because that leaves *microbie*, a feminine noun, to denote the state the *microbe* is in.'

Seeing them leaning towards each other like this, one might think: two clandestine militants of some tiny revolutionary group, possibly exchanging, in their coded language, dreams of better days to come. This is what fraternity must look like. The more impressed of the two is no doubt Calmette, face to face as he is with Alexandre Yersin, whose discovery of the diphtheria toxin places him in the front rank of scientists. Roux tipped him off in Paris. Yersin is an original, a loner who has gone off to play sailors or is it explorers? Calmette tells him that he has been given the job of establishing a Pasteur Institute here and suggests they work together. Yersin, caught on the hop, stiffens. The Pasteurian crowd is winding him in. Calmette has yet to find premises in Saigon. He hopes to open his research laboratory in a corner of the hospital.

For this purpose he has just joined the Colonial Health Corps, which counts as army. So there is an element of intimidation in what Roux and Pasteur cooked up in Paris. Yersin hesitates, afraid that one of these days he is going to have to regularise his position with the French authorities. He applied for naturalisation but has never done military service. However, all that is behind him now. That was his former life. Yersin rises, and the two shake hands. They may never meet again. Yet there is something here that might soon blossom into friendship, they can feel it. 'He tried everything to persuade me to join his Corps, but yesterday's arguments still hold today, so I've yet to make up my mind.'

Leaving the lounge of the Majestic, Yersin walks in the direction of the Messageries office, hands in pockets. It is not far, just along the embankment. He passes the Thu Ngu, the Semaphore Mast fixed with stays, and crosses a little bridge over the arroyo. Climbing aboard the *Volga*, he resumes his duties, rings the bell. Calmette returns to his room upstairs. Neither man yet knows how closely their lives will be linked.

Their correspondence will last for more than forty years. Captain Nègre has the *banca* winched up on deck. Yersin goes back to his life of exploring and his ambitions as an adventurer.

At sea, as evening comes, he possibly feels that hesitation still. He recalls the plans Calmette talked of. Studying the alcoholic fermentation of rice, the analgesic effects of opium, using venoms to cure otherwise fatal snake bites. Calmette was successful, that we know. When, later, the BCG vaccine is named, the central 'C' will be his initial. Today, there is the Calmette Hospital in Phnom Penh, not far from Wat Phnom and the city's Pasteur Institute. He worked hard to spread such establishments all over the globe as if by schizogenesis or metastasis. Before opening the one in Lille, he set up the first two Pasteur Institutes outside France. Or rather, outside the mother country. Because at the time Saigon, Lille and Algiers all counted as France.

in flight

This is still the case in May '40. Even if there is a feeling that this eight-day walkover by Nazi armies bodes ill for the survival of the Empire. This is the third time in less than a century that France has been invaded. The old man of seventy-seven, white of beard and blue of eye, dozes in the aircraft as it flies over the Mediterranean. Two days out from Marseilles, LeO H-242 takes off once more, from Athens aerodrome. The little white whale vibrates in the wide blue sky, leaving Cyprus beneath its left wing, amid the ambient drone of its four new-model Gnome & Rhône engines mounted atop an aerodynamic stack behind the cockpit.

Yersin notes down the information: Gnome & Rhône.

In Paris he attended what will be the last Congress of Pasteur Institutes for some time. He received the researchers' farewells in the gravelled courtyard, where Roux's tomb stands. Calmette and Roux have been dead for seven years. He saluted the departed, then shook hands with Joseph Meister, the first man saved from rabies, now sixty-four years of age.

Yersin no doubt wonders why he himself is still alive. How many more wars must he live through? He is reminded of the two Calmette brothers – the elder, Gaston, the journalist, to whom Proust dedicated the start of his great novel, and the younger, Albert, whom he first saw at the Majestic in Saigon. Ten years on, Roux wrote to him: 'Calmette must arrange for us to meet Sarraut at his brother's place.' Sarraut, then a minister, was being thought of as the next governor general of Indochina. In the same letter, Roux noted: 'Nothing new at the Institute. Here people are preoccupied by the Franco-German talks about Morocco.'

The elder brother, Gaston Calmette, then editor-in-chief of *Le Figaro*, was gunned down at his desk by the wife of another minister, Caillaux. That was in spring '14, just prior to the assassination of Jaurès and the outbreak of war. Once again Yersin tried to flee all that filth of politics and be alone. Even though he never, his whole life long, managed to get away from the Institute and the little Pasteurian crowd.

His attention is caught by a white and ochre stripe above the uniform blue of the horizon. The mountains of Lebanon.

In the days of Henri Mouhot, the man who discovered the Angkor temples back in the sixtieth year of the previous century – the year when Pasteur launched his great battle against spontaneous generation and climbed up from Chamonix to the 'Sea of Ice' to take samples of clean air – back then, travelling to Asia still involved a long detour round the Cape of Good Hope. Three months under sail. Thirty years on, Yersin's first voyage on board the *Oxus* was by steam through the Suez Canal and took no more than thirty days. Now, in spring '40, it is an eight-day flight. In the span of a lifetime the pumpkin has become first a melon, then a tangerine.

In the six years that he has been a regular guest of Air France he has learnt the stanzas of the aerial poem that he is now ticking off one by one: after Athens comes Beirut, then Damascus, Baghdad, Bushire, Jask, Karachi, Jodhpur, Allahabad, Calcutta, Rangoon, Bangkok, Angkor and Saigon. Over a dozen take-offs and landings since leaving Paris. Stages like hops of a flea.

At full throttle, the little white whale made of anodised Duralumin flies at two hundred kilometres an hour. Slower than today's trains. But an incredible speed then, a speed that makes the world beneath the cabin, when flown over at low altitude, seem to Yersin to be literally spinning round.

He always has to know everything, Yersin. His memory for places, names, just as for numbers, is insatiable. He records times, the pilot's name (Couret) and that of the flight engineer (Pouliquen), the state of the sky, of meteors, he rereads old notebooks or, bored, goes through the motions of taking notes. A compulsive explorer and researcher, he has filled hundreds of journals in his life. Let me, the ghost of the future, slip into the seat beside him, let me read over his shoulder, copy things down in my moleskin-covered notebook. This page, for instance, which might describe the trajectory of a spy drone anticipating an invasion of Iran:

Jask – dep. 0:55 hours. Alt. 1,000m.

1:50h – Pirate Point? Mouth of Persian Gulf.

2h – Small villages on rocks lining shore. Colour of sea emerald green close in. Palm groves. Small boats. Colour of rocks: grey.

3h – Barren peninsula with villages and palm groves. Boats on sea.

3:40h – Less barren open country to east. Nmrs villages (Chira), virtually midway between Jask and Bushire.

5h – Flew at 1,000m over plains or mountains close together. Nmrs villages. Virtually dry riverbed running NW to SE. Communication route.

5:30h – Broad valley running SE with large river.
   Chessboard of farmland.
6:30h – Arrival at Bushire, temp = 27°.

*

During those first few days of June '40, at each stop people try to get news, worrying about the military situation. They hear that the Allies have re-embarked their defeated troops at Dunkirk. The French ports are under bombardment. In St Nazaire, thousands of evacuees died when fire ravaged the Cunard liner *Lancastria*. Britain now faces Germany alone. Italy has entered the war.

Each day carries Yersin farther from the European inferno. At Calcutta, light stains the Ganges blood-red. He sees the web of purple and gold that is the delta at sunset. He is impatient to reach Nha Trang. He may well die on the flight and be buried where the plane happens to halt next. Instead of a basilica, an Institute will be built there. He counts the days and the take-offs like a schoolboy as summer approaches. He has been returning to Nha Trang regularly for almost fifty years now, and that is where he wants to die. Nya Trang, it is pronounced, as he points out in his letters, explaining to correspondents that Alexandre de Rhodes, author of the seventeenth-century *Portuguese–Annamite–Latin Dictionary*, was a Jesuit from Avignon and hence used the *langue d'oc* and the palatised 'h'. Nya Trang.

He always has to know everything, Yersin.

*

He owes it to the friendship of another Messageries Maritimes captain, Captain Flotte from St Nazaire, that he was able to discover Nha Trang.

And set foot in paradise.

Haiphong

In the navy, one goes where one is posted. The company having decided that serving the Philippines is no longer profitable, after a year aboard the *Volga* on the Manila run, Yersin is transferred to the new Haiphong line as doctor on the *Saigon*, a ship half the size.

The *Saigon* is a modest mixed cargo vessel carrying thirty-six passengers, slowly plying the South China Sea and the Gulf of Tonkin between Saigon and Haiphong. Never more than a day or night at sea. A cosy billet. Little tub sailing up and down the coast of Indochina or huge liner crossing the high seas: maritime law requires them all to carry a doctor wearing a white uniform with five gold stripes. The very occasional whitlow or migraine. Only Captain Flotte, with his waxy complexion behind a miasma of pipe smoke, causes Yersin any concern. The skipper himself gives a shrug. He has been knocking about this part of the world for ages, he is clearly immortal. So there is little for Yersin to do.

'We hug the coast, averaging two or three miles offshore, as a result of which we have a constantly changing landscape before our eyes. I have taken to sketching the profiles of mountains we pass, then I shall know where we are on the next trip. The captain has told me to do my scribbling from the bridge, asking me to give him copies afterwards, because the charts of this region are extremely poor.'

For the ten years that have passed since Jules Ferry ordered the French fleet under Admiral Courbet, with Loti among his officers, to seize Annam and Tonkin, only the coastal strip has been known to the French. If the two provinces are to be joined to Cochinchina by land, one day they will need to be mapped. This commercial shipping line, recently started up, is as yet the sole link between the two colonial capitals of Saigon and Hanoi. Each morning the doctor passes the lanyard of his navy binoculars around his neck and takes out his pencils and sketch block. The passengers, at an equally loose end, have slipped into British habits; the wealthiest have become posh, booked cabins to the left of the ship, the port side, on leaving Saigon and to starboard when sailing from Haiphong. Only Captain Flotte and Yersin, up on the bridge, enjoy a panoramic view.

On both outward and return journeys, the ship drops anchor deep inside a calm, sunny inlet. Davits are activated, boats lowered into the water, rowlocks set, and a few chests delivered to a fishing village. 'The first stop after Saigon is Nha Trang. It takes twenty-four hours to get there.' Yersin sketches very green coconut palms evidently swaying in the wind and sand that has a sparkling look. 'Ours is the only large vessel lying at anchor in that splendid bay.'

From Nha Trang the ship sails north, with the sky becoming progressively greyer, until it reaches the mouth of the Red River and the port of Haiphong. There, junks embark the passengers and take them on to Hanoi. Yersin buys a small boat and, as in Manila and Saigon, resumes his two-way freshwater trips up and down the branches of the delta. A week later, back the ship sails towards the sun and the south. Yersin rings the consultation bell. 'The passengers are a bit of a bore at times, but that is one of the miseries of existence.' Occasionally, there will be tall white colonial wives aboard, like sweat-beaded mares, threatening to faint from the heat. But it is Captain Flotte himself who is far from well and sometimes has to clutch at rails. Not the sort to put on airs, the skipper, more one to shrug and relight his pipe. If Yersin pronounces him sick, they may well put him ashore. Even if it means kicking the bucket, he would rather do so at sea. The pair become friends, then accomplices. Yersin provides the *Saigon* with a Chamberland water filter.

Calling at Nha Trang each time and each time finding it so magnificent, Yersin asks Flotte's permission to accompany the sailors as they make their delivery. He is dazzled by the vegetation in the hinterland, where the peaks of misty mountains rising some fifty kilometres off dominate the landscape. In the evenings, over drinks in the wardroom, the two resume their chats. No one, so far as is known at the time, has ever crossed or indeed mapped the range. Realising that here is a man whose future does not lie at sea, and aware that he risks losing his doctor, on the occasional trip the captain bends the rules to allow Yersin to stay in Nha Trang. Yersin crisscrosses the region, training himself to walk without shoes, though this is not yet exploration. He trains on the bridge as well, learning from the old skipper how to use a sextant and take bearings. At night he studies geodesy in his cabin, acquiring the knowledge of mathematics he needs for astronomical observations.

On this monotonous Saigon–Haiphong line with its tedious toing and froing, Yersin, thanks to Captain Flotte, lays the groundwork for his future as a cartographer and explorer. Homage is due to brave seaman Flotte, one of the thousands of courageous tars who have passed into oblivion. In fact, let us now praise Captain Flotte of St Nazaire.

A lifetime on the water, sailing all the world's seas and all the world's oceans to fetch up finally, having started from his birthplace of St Nazaire, in Bordeaux, where he dies in the Hospital for Tropical Diseases.

a doctor for the poor

After Calmette comes Loir. Yersin has a powerful sense that they are not going to let go of him now. Adrien Loir is Pasteur's own nephew. One of the leading lights of the little Pasteurian crowd. He and Yersin are the same age and worked as lab assistants together in rue Vauquelin before the rue Dutot buildings went up. At his uncle's suggestion, Loir sends Yersin telegram after telegram at the company's offices in Saigon, missives that Yersin receives each time the ship docks.

Loir has been sent to Australia to set up a Pasteur Institute there and try to wipe out the invasive rabbits, using the chicken cholera bacillus. He is also vaccinating dogs and dingoes against rabies and sheep against anthrax. Seriously overstretched, he wants his former fellow-student to come and help him. Yersin has always talked of 'moving on', seeking wider horizons, and here is Loir, offering him a more exciting life than coastal navigation in the South China Sea, more money than a ship's doctor makes, a laboratory in which to conduct his own research. Australia is a booming continent where everything is modern. They even have kangaroos. Loir leaves no stop unpulled.

Walking past the Majestic, Yersin turns up rue Catinet, enters the Gustave Eiffel Post Office and at the counter asks for a blue telegram slip. After the usual formalities, assuring Loir of his friendship and praising his achievements, he says he will not be coming to Sydney. Just as he rejected Calmette's proposition here in Saigon, which the latter is still waving under his nose. 'Calmette keeps on and on at me to join the colonial navy, promising me the earth if I agree.'

It is Yersin's conviction that the heyday of bacteriology already lies behind them. The age of the adventurer is over. The brilliant amateur working alone is a thing of the past. 'In my view, microbiology has reached the point where any major step forward will be a thoroughly tedious affair in which there will be many setbacks and miscalculations.' He has no wish to be one of those suffering such tedium. He is still young, Yersin, and he is in a hurry. He bores easily. Having learnt to walk barefoot through jungle, he is loath to go back to the footwear of the sedentary researcher. He left Paris precisely to avoid working indoors. He means to become an explorer. It was the career he chose even before becoming a doctor. He wrote as much to Fanny from Berlin, and now he reminds her. 'I shall inevitably, I can see, end up in scientific exploration. It simply holds too much appeal for me and, as you surely remember, that was always my inmost dream: to follow in the footsteps of Livingstone.'

And Livingstone, dead for some twenty years at this time, is a man he knows all about. The Scot's expedition from South Africa to Angola, then all the way across the continent to Mozambique. His habit of practising medicine in the villages he passed through. The discovery of the Zambesi River and the tireless quest for the sources of the Nile. The meeting on the shore of Lake Tanganyika with the journalist Stanley, who had been sent out to find him. *Doctor Livingstone, I presume?* His refusal to return with Stanley. His death a year later. How his faithful servants Shuma and Susi, having gutted his corpse and buried the entrails at the foot of a tree, had carried the dried body, slung from a pole between them, as far as Bagamoyo on the shore of the Indian Ocean before handing it over to the British at Zanzibar. The funeral service in Westminster Abbey, with Stanley holding the cords of the pall. *Here rests David Livingstone. Missionary. Traveller. Philanthropist.* Until Yersin, like his hero, discovers unknown lands, he will practise medicine for the poor of Nha Trang, each time he stops there.

'You ask me if I enjoy medical practice. Yes and no. I take great pleasure in treating those who come to me for advice, but I should not like to make medicine my living. You see, I could never ask a patient to pay me for the treatment I have been able to administer. I regard medicine as a sacerdotal office, like the priesthood. Demanding payment for treating an invalid is rather like saying, "Your money or your life."' Yersin continues to sail on the *Saigon*, and Messageries Maritimes pays him a salary, which for the moment means that he need not charge for consultations. His whole life long he will seek to evade economic as well as political ties. A loyal member of the Free Evangelical Church of Morges and follower of the example of Livingstone, himself a doctor, explorer and shepherd of his sheep.

At length, in that spring of '40, he alights at Nha Trang station and returns home to Fishermen's Point, Xom Con, for after the eight-day flight and the dozen or so take-offs and landings and the farewell to the little white whale of anodised Duralumin, now beached at Saigon airport, it is by train that the old whitebeard regains the imposing, peaceful bay. He takes a leisurely stroll along the jetty, and fishermen greet him. These are the grandsons of the fishermen who greeted him originally. This is the last homecoming of good

Dr Nam, as they call him here – or Uncle Five for the five gold stripes on his white uniform, even though he has not worn that uniform since the previous century, when he was the dashing sailor, black of beard and blue of eye, who treated their grandparents.

He enters his big square seafront house. He designed it himself, years ago. A cube, totally rational. Up on the roof, the dome of his astronomical observatory. Each of its three floors is ringed by a colonnaded gallery with arched openings. This time his staff feared they might never see him again. He unpacks his suitcase and lines up the pharmaceutical products that he is going to have to use sparingly from now on. Later, he sits in his rocking chair on the veranda, gazing out to sea. The play of sunlight in palm trees, and all around the magnificent bay. Near by the noisy, multicoloured aviaries, beside him his parrot.

In the morning, he listens to the wireless to catch the evening news from Paris. The voice of the Marshal, dedicating himself to France and preparing to sign the shameful armistice. France is defeated. Switzerland is neutral. Germany triumphant. The French campaign, lasting only days, cost two hundred thousand lives, the toll of a single epidemic. Hence the French name for it: the 'Brown Death'. He well knows that the war, being a world war, will eventually reach Nha Trang. One day, Germany's Japanese allies will come ashore at Fishermen's Point. As an elderly epidemiologist, Yersin has learnt to rely on the worst always happening.

It's very risky, growing old.

For some, it actually helps to die young and handsome. Had gangrene not taken him, Arthur Rimbaud would now be only two years younger than Pétain. Yersin is seventy-seven. Back in Nha Trang, he resumes his monastic existence. He will not leave the big square house until the day of his death, whenever that may be. He feels a moment's hesitation. What adventure shall he throw himself into at this biblical age? He knows his days are numbered. For a long time now people have been urging him to write his memoirs. The Pasteur crowd. Without really getting down to it, he is starting to go through old trunks, putting his legacy in some sort of order. However, only rereading his old exploration notebooks, when what they are asking for is that he tell, yet again, the big story: bubonic plague.

Yersinia pestis.

the long march

Yersin, at twenty-nine, is keen to drop science, he's done with all that, microbiology, research, he has changed direction, chosen the sea, known the bliss of wharves and cranes, dawn embarkations, the way big ships move, the song of evening on the gentle yellow Asian waves. But, two years at sea and already he's bored. He loves the precision of naval language and the thrill of great seaports described by that other Swiss, Cendrars, but he cannot imagine growing old on the bridge like good Captain Flotte. He asks Messageries Maritimes to let him go. They agree. So here he is, set free not only by the Institute but also by the shipping line.

Whatever he takes up, he will be accused of fickleness.

Behind him, there are his works on tuberculosis and diphtheria. He is a scientist whom Pasteur once marked out for
great things, he is also an excellent ship's doctor. Yersin has
already contrived to stop people hassling him.

With his time now his own, he leaves Saigon and goes to live
in Nha Trang, first having a little place built for himself at
Fishermen's Point, Xom Con, where he opens a surgery of
sorts. Dr Nam is the first Western doctor in the area. With no
money coming in, he tries (not really believing it will work)
to initiate a system of paid consultations for the local bigwigs
who can afford it while continuing to treat the poor for nothing (never really managing to distinguish the two groups),
and he resumes his training ventures.

He covers hundreds of kilometres in the hills, sleeps in
Moi villages, makes something of a study of their languages,
goes hunting with Moi tribesmen and treats their ailments.
He has the idea of one day organising vaccination cam-
paigns. For the present, he learns how to handle spear and
crossbow, in exchange introducing his teachers, much to their
amusement, to the rudiments of his multi-bladed Swiss
penknife. And every now and then he returns to Nha Trang.
'My Annamite patients congregate from all corners, the
minute I am back. The truth is, they tend to be the ones that
benefit more than I do from my medical skills when, to pay
me, they do me the kindness of filching my wallet. But what

can one do, they have this notion that robbing a Frenchman constitutes a good deed. And why are the French in Indochina at all if it is not to steal from the Annamites?'

Before his small stock of savings evaporates, he uses it to buy equipment and mounts his first proper expedition. After the sea and the open forest, he wants to traverse the jungle and climb the mountains rising ever higher beyond. Lacking an official sponsor, he makes do with the support of Moi tribesmen, who agree to act as his guides on the early stages. Leaving Nha Trang and the South China Sea coast behind him, he plans to cross the mountain range and rejoin the Mekong River on the other side. He will not be seen again for some time, maybe never. With him he takes an interpreter and five men to open up a route. He bards his torso with leather harnesses holding his marine chronometer and his theodolite. Slung across his back is a Winchester – for hunting, he hopes. Having purchased horses and two elephants, he strikes out in a north-westerly direction. Each stage will be a three-hour walk.

This time he does go straight ahead, forbidding himself any turning back. They advance in the saddle for preference, to avoid leeches, leading the horses along tracks, then hauling them by the bridle when there is no longer a track. The bulky elephants follow behind, and for them it is necessary to slash a path through the bamboos and shrubbery. The tribesmen turned back long ago. Insects cling to his clothing that would have been discoveries even to his father.

In the evening they treat themselves to a little rice whisky by way of a tonic, fires are lit, mosquito nets hung, flutes taken out. Next day, as they come to a village, unlike Mayréna, later King Marie I, who handed out lead shot, they distribute ointments and any spare quinine. Following each bivouac, the instruments and photographic equipment are carefully packed up, with a piece of waterproof canvas to protect them from rain. Embers are extinguished and the elephants' packsaddles loaded. The party advances, straight ahead. Into unnamed territory peopled by fearsome tribes who know nothing of violins or alexandrines. A ship's compass keeps them on course. Here at last is real freedom, the truly pure life. Opening up paths, forging into the unknown, be it towards God or towards oneself. The laughable riddle of self. The enigma he could never resolve in the dim light of a Protestant temple back in Vaud.

Phnom Penh

Having crossed passes more than two thousand metres up, they descend through chill fir forests, then steamy jungles, towards the shattered lattice of rice paddies visible far below. The handful of exhausted marchers reach the Mekong in the vicinity of Stung Treng three months after leaving Nha Trang. Yersin sells off the elephants and horses and puts his little troop aboard a long pirogue. After covering the whole distance on foot at the head of his caravan in order to avoid disturbing his chronometer, he can at last sit down and be borne along by the current of the immensely wide, jade-green river.

*

What was then called quai Piquier, running beside the wet dock (long since filled in), is now 108th Street, not far from Wat Phnom and the French quarter, the Royal Hotel, and today's Pasteur Institute and Calmette Hospital. However, when Yersin first arrives at Phnom Penh, it is still a large village. Following his three-month march, he presents himself to the French authorities. A reception is organised by the Resident-Superior of Cambodia, Louis Huyn de Verneville, a full-dress dinner, in all probability, with local notables attending and ceiling fans revolving overhead. Our Vaudois fails to share this illogical predilection of the regicide French for the lees of the aristocratic system that have settled in banking or the diplomatic service. One sinks, on such occasions, into armchairs upholstered with buffalo hide.

Yersin is the first traveller to link the coast of Annam to Cambodia by land. The only known way of accessing the Kingdom of the Khmers at this time is by river. Servants in traditional costume serve champagne. He is questioned about his journey through areas unknown and about his encounters with savages, both male and female. However, Yersin's conversation, when he deigns to open his mouth, is as scientific as his letters.

'Wherever I could, I took bearings: almost all my latitudes were determined by a series of Polar Star elevations, an excellent procedure because repeating the observation makes the results more precise. I can guarantee them to within 20 degrees. My longitudes will of course depend on whether my chronometer is fast or slow: I checked it each time I had to spend several days in one place, and I found it regular enough to enable me to guarantee my longitudes to within 4 degrees.'

This is René Char's 'useful poetry'. It soon becomes a bore. Guests are impervious to this literature that will succeed Romanticism. They inspect the blades of the fan or the toes of their polished shoes, accept fresh glasses of champagne, light cigarettes. Through the tall windows they watch the golden waters of the Tonle Sap as they flow into the Mekong, the bonzes in their orange robes as they process up to Wat Phnom pagoda. Yersin too is bored, and the dinner draws to a close. Absinthe time. The idea of giving a ball in his honour is quietly abandoned.

No skin off his nose, he has no patience with any of it. He cannot understand why people applaud him and offer congratulations. Exploration is simple, like diphtheria. All it involves is keeping both eyes open and both legs moving – heaving one's carcass out of the buffalo-hide armchair, in other words. Mathematicians are notoriously amazed to discover that not all those around them can solve the simplest cubic equation. Yet their amazement is quite sincere. People mistake for arrogance what is mere naivety. Such men are surprised to find out that not everyone is their equal. For them, it rocks the foundations of the Republic that people should more readily accept the proposition that not any Tom, Dick or Harry can run a hundred metres in ten seconds. They are like hypermnesiacs, irked by encountering proof that, as a rule, people forget things pretty fast.

Yersin and his little troop regain Saigon via a riverboat that plies the waters of the Mekong delta. He draws up a report recording his ethnological and geographical observations, illustrating it with nearly a hundred and fifty photographs developed in his Nha Trang shack. He draws detailed maps of his journey. These are sent to Luang Prabang in Laos, where they are appended to the findings of the Pavie Mission. The text is sent off to Paris. There is nothing picturesque about the text. It has the precision of a Pasteurian summary, a paean of praise to his Swiss chronometer, a Vacheron model, and to his barometer, 'checked against that of the Manila Observatory'.

The account is too scientific even for the popular French periodical *Le Tour du monde*. No attacks by tigers, no languorous native princess with pointy breasts. Without going into detail, the newspapers of the mother country nevertheless tell a tale of prowess. Yersin is invited to Paris. Pasteur insists on making available his old room at the Institute, welcoming him back to the bosom of the family. The Lutetia has yet to be built. His expedition report is published in the journal of the French Geographical Society, which five years earlier published Arthur Rimbaud's account of his African exploration under the title *Rapport sur l'Ogadine*, today's Ogaden. In boulevard St Germain, Yersin enters the premises of the Geographical Society, passing between two caryatids that support, respectively, earth and sea.

Seated side by side at his lecture are the little rue Dutot crowd and the little rue Mazarine crowd, the Pasteurian scientists – among them Émile Roux himself, fresh from extinguishing his Bunsen burner and hanging his white coat on a peg in the lobby – and the explorer-geographers, whose ranks include Auguste Pavie in person, back from Laos and from his Luang Prabang vice-consulate. Astonishment is shown at the young man's skill in straddling the two communities, much as in the next century Paul Gégauff will link the cinematic *nouvelle vague* crowd and the literary *nouveau roman* crowd. Journalists, who to serve their papers' need to shift copies tend always to favour caricature and the facial quirk, are curious to know what the fellow looks like. They are in for a disappointment. Neither the stare of the mad scientist nor the glare of a firebrand. A calm, determined young man with a clear blue gaze and a well-trimmed black beard. 'That evening I dined at Mr Pasteur's, a man who much enjoys travel yarns.' It was the young concierge, Joseph Meister, then aged sixteen, who let him in and took his coat.

Yersin stays in Paris for three months, enrolling in a course at the Montsouris Observatory. Having no income currently, he throws himself into the search for backers and for funds to prepare fresh expeditions. But he refuses to become involved in the Pavie Mission. He knows his Caesar. Better to be first in Nha Trang than second in Luang Prabang. Once again he turns to Pasteur for support. This letter is quite different, sounding much more enthusiastic than the one to Messageries Maritimes.

Dr Yersin asks me to commend his request to the Minister of Foreign Affairs. It is with every confidence and the keenest zeal that I do so. Dr Yersin worked at the Pasteur Institute for two years with enormous success. He and Dr Roux produced a first-class paper on diphtheria together: his wide knowledge of medicine fully earned him the title of doctor. He could have had a brilliant future as a scientist. However, all of a sudden, having read widely, he was overcome by a burning desire to travel, and nothing would keep him with us. I can vouchsafe that Dr Yersin is among the most genuine of men, thoroughly decent, possessed of exceptional courage, endowed with qualities as varied as they are specific – someone, in short, capable of doing great honour to our country. Moreover, simply perusing the enclosed report of his recent journey to the Mekong will instantly convey to the most exalted degree Dr Yersin's qualities as a traveller and explorer.

His hope is that such a reference will yield a tidy sum. It yields pence.

During this first stay in Europe since going to sea, Yersin visits Morges, gives Fanny a hug, acquires from Vacheron, with the small sum his efforts did in fact produce, a new chronometer and electrometer, together with several thermometers, and from chez Mayor buys a brace of hunting rifles and some cartridges. Seated in the little chintz lounge at Fig Tree House, surrounded by a gaggle of gossip columnists as well as by Fanny and the young ladies of good family, he spreads out his explorer's notebooks, which soon, as we know, make tedious reading. What about pictures? Yersin shows his photographs of Moi women, which Fanny hastily covers with a table-mat. Whereupon the young ladies blush reliably, just as their lessons have taught them. Still, when all is said and done, this is her Alexandre, who as a boy sang psalms at the Free Evangelical Church and is now snapping Negresses with nothing on.

a new Livingstone

From that point on, this is Yersin's life: explorer and land surveyor, by appointment to the governor general, the man now standing beside him in a Saigon office, both of them poring over enigmatic, wildly imaginative portulans of Annam, Tonkin and Laos, pencil in hand. The land they inhabit is conquered but unknown. Roman generals after the Battle of Alésia, examining a primitive sketch of Gaul and Germania. Speculating where there might be minerals, even perhaps gold, in what they are looking at, where to establish towns, to station troops. Just like ourselves, like all conquerors, children dreaming before coloured maps, atlases: Harlequin's cloak thrown down upon the world to interpret it.

Yersin is back from Phnom Penh, back from Paris, back from consulting manuscripts in the library of the Geographical Society, the few, slightly exalted reports of missionaries, his mind planning the routes of future expeditions. He misses it a bit, of course, bacteriology, much as he misses being at sea. His urge to discover is encyclopaedic.

For the space of two years he fulfils his mission. He is given supplies and men and money and weapons. In exchange, he is asked to investigate, as he goes, possible new routes for commerce, note places suitable for rearing stock, assess timber and mineral resources. It is the traditional Saint-Simonian idea of exploiting the wealth of the planet. One day, of course, it will be necessary to invent the pneumatic tyre as well, and above it the articulated lorry to speed up extraction. This is back in the day when nature is still something man must master and possess. When nature, now a fragile old crock in need of protection, was a redoubtable foe to be subdued.

At nightfall, in camp, Yersin lays maps across his knees, marks streams that, come monsoon time, will turn into torrents of mud and need to be bridged. He journeys as far as the Cham villages, penetrating the ancient civilisation of the Champa people, distant descendants of the Malays and predecessors of the Khmers and Annamites, because all invaders, once settled, are themselves subject to invasion. For two years he knows cold, astringent dawns among the peaks of the cordillera. In the jungle, at night, fires burn at the camp perimeter to ward off wild animals. Days of hunting across grasslands and bouts of malaria, chill fevers beneath warm rains. Endless discussions with the rice whisky passed around, amulets and exchanges of blood from cuts in the forearm – not a particularly Pasteurian custom, but Yersin carries with him magical, antiseptic Pasteurian products devised by Calmette in Saigon.

The exploration business grows and grows. At the core of each expedition: elephants and small saddle horses. Around them: animals to roast on the journey, baskets of poultry, porters and scouts. On occasion, a line of eighty people winds through the trees. We have a photograph of Yersin, a self-portrait, showing him in a wide bush hat and a Chinese jacket buttoned up to the collar. Palm fronds part before him as he halts for a moment to position the big shiny wooden cube on its tripod. Stop. Freeze-frame. Let's list the materials he is wearing or carrying about his person: plant fibre for the clothing, metal and glass for the instruments, leather and bits of tanned animal hide for the belt and harnesses, all known of since ancient times, as are the horse and elephant; no plastic yet, no synthetic fibre. Play. Yersin resumes his progress and the curtain of palms closes behind him.

During this second expedition, having scaled a conifer-clad

mountain, they find themselves scanning a vast grassy plateau that stretches to the horizon, the entire location lying above one thousand metres and extremely cold. Cutting through the middle, a river. The vision is pure Switzerland. On his return, Yersin writes that 'the sight was reminiscent of a sea convulsed by a heaving swell of green undulations'.

He has discovered the Lang Bian Plateau.

And four years later Paul Doumer, the new governor general, having read Yersin's report, decides to gain an idea of the place for himself. Doumer is keen to create, in Indochina, a high-altitude station for weary colonials and malaria sufferers, a combination of convalescent home and sanatorium. The two men, with a small team around them, undertake the climb.

Paul Doumer is the emblematic black-frockcoated public servant of the Third Republic and of democratic egalitarianism. Brought up by his mother, a widowed housekeeper, this man of slender means rises from worker to teacher to member of parliament. Joining the ranks of the radical left, he promotes development of the sciences and of health education. He decides to found a pretty alpine village in the cool climate of Lang Bian.

The pair, the orphan from Morges and the orphan from Aurillac, remain friends until Doumer's death.

It is a lengthy friendship, for Doumer's career will itself be long and brilliant. Culminating in the office of President of the Republic, it eventually, in '32, sees him cut down by a number of shots from the revolver of Russian émigré Pavel Gorguloff. This is long after the assassinations, likewise by firearm, of Calmette's brother in his *Figaro* office and Jaurès in his local. Filthy business, politics.

Dalat

And forty years on, in the mid-Thirties, three years after Doumer's assassination, Yersin is still going strong and the place has become Dalat.

Edging the Lake, villas as in Normandy and Biarritz. Up in the hills, chalets just like those in Savoy. Banks of flowers, agapanthus and nasturtiums and hydrangeas, recalling Dinard. A rack railway climbs to the once unspoilt plateau, serving a station that, like the one at Pointe-Noire in Congo, is a copy of a building in Deauville. The Pasteur Institute runs the hospital. A convent has opened where nuns sing matins and lauds – the Convent of the Birds, it is called – and a high school accommodating several hundred students that the elderly Yersin, discoverer of the plateau, lets them name after him.

A reception has been organised by the new governor general in the panelled interior of Lang Bian Palace, set in a park of cedars, pines and araucarias that runs down in a gentle slope to the lakeshore. Emperor Bao Dai, whose summer residence is near by, where he lodges briefly when not at the casino in Monaco, uses the ceremony as an opportunity to present old man Yersin with the Grand Cross of the Order of the Dragon of Annam.

Perched at the shiny, curved bar, facing the hotel's reading room beyond the marble columns, the ghost of the future listens to what the emperor of cheap show in his white suit and co-respondent shoes is saying. In the hearth, a blazing fire. Tapestries, gilt decorations, curtains and Chinese vases: all hauled up the mountain from the coast on the rack railway, which has also just disgorged the official delegation and the journalists, among whom the ghost of the future gained entry unnoticed.

When Dalat's Yersin High School opens in that year of '35, Yersin is seventy-two. They have tracked down and invited some very ancient Moi tribesmen whom Yersin encountered at the time of his trip, when there was nothing up here but green grass and game. Yersin too has been borrowed for the occasion, and in his black suit banded with the red and gold

Dragon sash he is somewhat embarrassed not to be able to say, in the presence of Emperor Bao Dai and the French and Annamite authorities who are all saying such flattering things about him, what he feels deep down. He liked the place better as it was before. That swelling expanse of grassland. He rather regrets discovering it, certainly he is sorry he ever disclosed its whereabouts to his friend Doumer. The plateau should have been left to the mountain tribes.

He reads his speech of thanks to the governor general and the emperor of cheap show, but in private that is in fact what he thinks. He is like that, Yersin, championing progress when he is the instigator of it but finding nostalgia creep up on him with age. Beneath the crystal chandeliers, with the piano beside him, the old man in the red and gold sash lays blue eyes on the blue waters of the Lake. A fleeting vision of Morges and Fig Tree House. He glimpses Doumer, of whom politics were indeed the death. Yet again, mid-Thirties Europe is approaching war. Here, people feign ignorance, clapping and raising glasses of champagne in this carefree Art Deco holiday village among stands of pine trees. He has already written to Calmette: 'I found Dalat transformed and on the way to becoming a modern city. You know me well enough to suspect that such improvements, however necessary, fail to delight me.'

A place he prefers is Dankia, a Moi village some dozen kilometres distant 'whose large smooth hillocks are swathed in green grass, with forest on the horizon, capping the highest hills, a sight that I find oddly reminiscent of the alpine pastures of the Jura'. As if in a dream, Yersin remembers the first time he crossed the deserted Lang Bian Plateau with its long green swell of tall wild grasses. He was still in his twenties. And ultimately, had Yersin died at that moment, not having written *Les Illuminations*, had he succumbed, back then, to the blows of the brigand Thouk, in the annals of medicine and of geography his life would have amounted to no more than this: having discovered the diphtheria toxin, effected an experimental form of tuberculosis in rabbits, traced a route from Annam to Cambodia and located a pretty spot to build a Swiss-style spa in Asia.

The ghost of the future, the scribe with the moleskin notebook who has been following Yersin since Morges, who put up at the Hotel Zur Sonne in Marburg, the Lutetia in Paris, the Royal in Phnom Penh, the Majestic in Saigon and is currently staying at the Lang Bian Palace in Dalat, says to himself it is rather nice, on the whole, following this fellow. The accommodation is tip-top. This afternoon he took a stroll down by the Lake. So, since the Thirties this town has grown up, spreading from nothing over the verdant plateau. Dalat has certainly changed since Yersin's day, changed masters, changed people, but the setting is still the same. Not unlike Bagnoles-de-l'Orne in Normandy or Cambo-les-Bains in the Basque country. Here, thirty years of warfare left no permanent impression, water off a duck's back, the fighting was a long way off. The scribe writes as much in his notebook spread open on the shiny wooden bar with, crowding around, journalists who have come by train from Hanoi and Saigon to cover the school opening. No one recognises him. He claims to be a special correspondent sent by *Paris-Soir*. They ask him for news of the home country. The gossip about Jean Gabin or Arletty. And whether the Popular Front looks like winning next year's elections. His replies are vague.

The ghost of the future makes not a single mistake. His attire is suitably timeless. Cotton trousers and white shirt, blue tie, stout leather brogues. He knows the news as if he had read it in the press archives the previous day. He is aware of the latest advances in science and technology, speaks French without any neologisms. A thoroughly prepared agent, planted back in the Thirties. He might feel very much like taking a Marlboro Light from his pocket, but he knows the brand does not exist yet. Perhaps, through overconfidence or over-indulgence in drink, he has neglected to switch off his mobile and takes the call?

They immediately crowd around his bar stool, there is a rumpus, someone rings the police. He is accused of being a spy, working for the Communist Party of Indochina, which Ho Chi Minh founded five years before this. The bodyguards form a ring around that lackey of imperialism, Emperor Bao

Dai. The elderly explorer in the Dragon sash is forgotten. At the police station it is worse, the ghost of the future confesses, tries to explain, ties himself in knots, makes predictions, the outbreak of the next world war in four years' time, the arrival of the Japanese, French soldiers in camps. General Giap, the rebel leader, in a suite of the Lang Bian Palace. Dien Bien Phu and the victory of Ho Chi Minh. The Vietnam War and the defeat of the Americans. The arrival of the Soviets. Men surround him, the injection, the straitjacket, the old song (slightly adapted): ' ... you'll not be back in Paris any time soon.'

Arthur & Alexandre

The mobile stayed silent. The ghost is back in his suite. He fills the cast-iron bathtub with the Ethiopian lion's feet, removes his tie, sets the brass fan going. On the desk, a book by Leonardo Sciascia with one sentence underlined: 'Notoriously, science, like poetry, is but one step from madness.'

On the bed, scattered notes. Letters to the two mothers, Vitalie and Fanny. To the two sisters, Isabelle and Émilie. Letters scrawled rapidly in which there is repeated mention of leaving, going away, buying a horse, or ordering something: a sextant, a theodolite, an aneroid barometer, treatises on engineering, textbooks on excavation, mineralogy, trigonometry, hydraulics, astronomy, chemistry. One man was assembling the largest scientific library in Annam, the other the largest scientific library in Abyssinia. The ghost might have written the lives of the two men in parallel. The long life of the one and the short life of the other.

The Lang Bian Palace is a small island of suspended time. Today it is called the Dalat Palace, without the change really reflecting the passage from capitalism to communism. It may be that, after independence, no one dared rename the hotel Ho Chi Minh Palace, after the man who spent much of his life in makeshift encampments, or even after one of his generals, General Giap, though Giap did stay there during the talks with the French.

The brass taps, nearly a hundred years old and now showing a greenish patina, still work. Persian carpets invariably lend themselves to transportation, both in time and space. To daydreaming, whether geographic or demographic. Stretching his limbs in the warm water, the ghost of the future lights a cigarette and listens to the wind as it ruffles the trees in the grounds. Seven billion people currently populate the globe. Whereas back at the beginning of the twentieth century it was under two. An estimated eighty billion humans have lived and died since the emergence of *Homo sapiens*. Not a lot. A simple sum: if we each wrote a mere ten Lives during the course of our own, no life would be forgotten. None would be erased. They would all attain posterity, and justice would be done.

A grave is nothing, but a tomb … Writing a Life is like playing the violin with a score in front of you. One man lived from the Second Empire to the Second World War, the other fell off his horse at thirty-seven. They shared the same frenzy for finding things out and 'moving on', leaving their little crowds behind them, one the Pasteurians, the other the Parnassians. A longing for sun-drenched dawns and for seagoing, for botany, for photography. 'I have just ordered, from Lyons, a camera that will enable me to intersperse this work with views of these strange lands.' That odd album about the country of the Galla – Yersin wrote one just like it about the country of the Moi. Both men, living in the back of beyond, gave off new ideas at the rate of one every five minutes. Importing Syrian mules into Ethiopia, cows from Normandy into Indochina. The adventure of science, 'the new nobility! Progress. The world marches on!' The love of mathematics. The sum of the angles of a triangle invariably equals two right angles. Poetry should be the same. The alexandrine that came to him at the end of a letter to Fanny. The line that could be completed by no matter what verb, because 'It is no way to live, not … '

As Yersin is mounting his expeditions, the other falls from his horse in Dire Dawa. Rimbaud's Greek friend Righas wrote that he had 'dislocated his knee and been gashed by a mimosa thorn'. The two shared a yearning for solitude, for going off somewhere, anywhere, always at the head of the caravan, for outdoing and outreaching their absent fathers. Going farther, in science and geography, than the fathers they had never known. For one, the microscope and scalpel found in the attic in Morges. For the other, the Koran and the Arabic grammar found in the attic in Roche. It was indeed a case of outdoing Captain Rimbaud of the little Saharan crowd when young Arthur opened up a route from Entoto to Harar. Just as it meant outdoing the 'Intendant of Powders', opening up a route from Nha Trang to Phnom Penh. As for the atrocious hot spells and parched throats, it was the women who learnt of those, the mother and sister who never left Switzerland or the Ardennes but sat at home reading letters bereft of forenames, signed bluntly, as the fathers' had been, *Rimbaud* in the one instance, *Yersin* in the other.

Not discovering the plague bacillus would have condemned the Morges man to die as one unknown explorer among thousands. All it took to kill the Roche man was a pricked finger, the stuff of fairy tales. But men's lives are like that: sublime heights, depths of absurdity. Curing plague, dying of gangrene.

into Sedang territory

If a prick from a needle or a mimosa thorn is an open door to death, the gaping red wound left by a spear thrust into a torso carves a great tunnel into which millions of microbes plunge. Yersin, knowing his medicine and his surgery, saves his own skin after the encounter with Thouk. Seldom do such lives not suffer a crisis of violence.

If all his years of exploration, coupled with his unstinting practice of medicine and vaccination of children, make Yersin resemble his peace-loving hero, the good Dr Livingstone, his intransigence and dark moods occasionally cause him to behave more like the quarrelsome Stanley. Firing at bands of brigands who at the time are called marauders and high-waymen but will later inspire the guerrilla groups led by the first anti-colonial fighters, men such as Mandrin and Lampião.

In this case it is Thouk, a tall bandit leader who roams the countryside, storming and pillaging, at the head of some fifty prison fugitives, alleged murderers with nothing to lose, desperate men with prices on their heads. They have the odd rifle, plundered from troops, some pikes, machetes. Yersin, visiting Moi friends, arrives at a village one evening to find it sacked, smoke still curling up from the ruins. The survivors point into the jungle, and the bravest come with him when, under cover of night, he sets off in pursuit. Thouk's men are hampered by the weight of the stolen rice and the slow pace of the cattle, also by their swaggering assurance that a few unarmed villagers will not dare to accost them in the forest, where evil spirits lurk. They halt, light fires, tally their booty. Yersin aims his revolver. The leaping flames project a whole theatre of shadows among the foliage. Thouk bounds, deflecting the barrel. Yersin takes a violent blow from a club that smashes his fibula. He falls to the ground, still fighting. A machete bites into his left thumb. Thouk drives a spear through his chest, and the gang flees, leaving him for dead. As would indeed have been the case for any one of those brigands, lacking as they did the magic products of the Pasteurians.

Yersin's men find him at dawn, bleeding but conscious beside the dying embers. Transfixed by the spear, like an insect on a card. That expedition comes to an abrupt end – as might Yersin's life have done. Ants and creepy-crawlies of various kinds are drinking from the reddened earth. Some explorers' careers leave their biographers in the lurch after only a couple of pages. Dozing supine with a crimson hole in the chest. Such Lives start and finish with a headline in some ghastly colonial rag, flung open by men sipping vermouths and cassis cocktails on the café terraces of rue Catinat: 'Discoverer of diphtheria toxin dies with spear through chest up in Moi country.'

Yersin, who has lost too much blood, knows that the clock is ticking and directs the procedure himself. On his advice the spear is not pulled out until the flesh has been cut away all around it. It is then slowly extracted without its tearing at the ribs. The main wound is sterilised, the others cleaned and disinfected, a bandage rolled tightly around the chest and another around the hand, and a splint strapped to the broken leg. He is laid on a stretcher made of lianas and bamboo that men bear on their shoulders for several days, eventually reaching Phan Rang. There a telegrapher (who one hopes is agoraphobic) lives alone in a hut beneath his post and its tangle of suspended black wires. A message is sent to Calmette in Saigon, asking him to restock the pharmacy.

Little by little, Yersin recovers. His biographer breathes

again. The patient keeps quite still for a few days, then resumes his notebook entries. 'In a way, the episode resulted, so far as I am concerned, in my losing a rifle and a revolver. I do not think I shall be held to account over it: the governor general will be highly displeased by this attempted rebellion in the South at a time when he is telling all and sundry that Annam is entirely subdued. So he will try to hush the affair up, even deny it happened if he has to. Anyway, I do not regret what I did: it was nothing short of my duty.'

While his wounds heal, Yersin (and again he cannot help it) delves into telegraphy. His leg encased in plaster, he is taken to Saigon, where he writes up his report, draws maps, marks where roads could be driven through and makes a fair copy of his notebook scribbles. The convalescent reads technical journals and writes to France, ordering fresh equipment. Down at the port, as soon as he is fit to travel, he is handed out of a victoria drawn there by tiny horses. Depositing his crutches in a cabin of the *Saigon*, bound for Haiphong, he has a chat with his successor on board, the man now wearing the white uniform with the five gold stripes. He disembarks at the first port of call, his beloved Nha Trang, exchanging the old Messageries tub for his wooden shack at Fishermen's Point.

There, limping busily to and fro in his darkroom, he develops his photographs. He is already preparing his next expedition, the longest on the map, due north, then west. The most ambitious, too. His intention: to open up a different route between Tonkin and Laos from Pavie's that goes via Dien Bien Phu. More letters to Fanny. 'I enclose a note for Mayor, asking him to supply me with new firearms, for which I shall let him have payment on receipt.'

Just before his departure he learns that Thouk has been arrested, and he reassures Fanny – or possibly worries her even more: 'I leave for the interior tomorrow, and I am loath to do so without telling you that my hand has healed up completely and my leg is quite better too. So I am in a fit state to continue my trip. Today they beheaded Thouk. I attended the execution to take a few pictures. It's a horrible business, actually. The head fell with the fourth blow of the sword. And Thouk did not flinch. These Annamites die with a calm resignation that is truly impressive.'

In France, that year brings the centenary of the Reign of Terror, when quite a few heads rolled too, rolled and dropped into baskets. No one feels like commemorating it with a second iron tower. That same year the French fleet sails out of Saigon to blockade Bangkok at the behest of Pavie, now elevated to 'Frontier Commissioner'. No risk of Yersin becoming a diplomat. Filthy business, politics.

He presses on with a forced march into Sedang country. Yet another expedition tramps across jungle clearings and winds through misty pine forests, meeting those columns of millions of ants whose advance nothing will divert by so much as a metre and before which villagers have no choice but to give up and relocate. Up in the mountains, the group of guides and beasts of burden climb tracks along ledges, ford torrents. Riding at Yersin's side is Father Guerlach, who has just made the earliest topographical and anthropological surveys of the region and recorded the beliefs and idioms of its hunter-gatherers in the vague hope of saving their souls rather than reducing them to slavery, as Mayréna, known locally as King Marie I, had tried to do – with little success, it has to be said.

The haunts of the Sedang are eyries atop peaks, protected by tall stockades. As soon as Guerlach is recognised, pulley-operated gates are opened, friendly greetings offered, objects exchanged, dances performed, meals shared. In the centre of the arena, Yersin sets out his scientific instruments. Legs apart, eyes upraised, he takes latitudes and longitudes, finds the Pole Star at night, measures altitudes with the aid of his barometer. Father Guerlach unpacks crucifixes and censers, says mass, mumbles prayers, and stretches out arms towards his god, who apparently lodges somewhere near the Pole Star. For some of the Sedang, this is their first encounter with men wilder than themselves, their first chance to observe such priceless rituals. They roar with laughter, slap their thighs. The witch doctors gather on one side and huff, though later, without fail, they incorporate versions of the display in their own ceremonies. Up on the ramparts, warriors brandish shields covered in rhino hide, yelling and shaking spears and swords to wish the White Men a safe return. The column goes down the mountain, eventually reaching Attapeu in Laos, on the far side of the range. This time the attraction for villagers lies in the sight, quite new to them, of domesticated horses in full harness.

The explorers descend gentle, jungle-covered slopes towards the banks of the Mekong. They have been on the go for months now. Their progress is silent and exhausting. Beneath their feet, yellow and pale green, emerald green and violet. Through branches overhead, a large, lemon-yellow sun and tall palms threshing in the rain squalls. Snakes and frogs and tiny protective spirits that scuttle away. The sudden squawking of red budgerigars taking flight. They turn north and cross passes once more, subsequently heading due east towards the sea to hit Tourane. Then on to Hanoi, where the two anthropologists, the Catholic and the agnostic, deliver their reports to the bishop and the governor respectively. Numbers are inscribed in pen and ink on the bones and enemy skulls offered as gifts by the Sedang and on elephant tusks collected on the trip. Chests are filled with ethnological knick-knacks for dispatch to the Museum of Mankind in Paris.

It is all a bit like signing the ship's log in the wardroom before disembarking. For Yersin, this has become an activity not so very different from, if more exciting than, navigation.

He shows no sign of weariness. He makes arrangements to return to Nha Trang via the Messageries Maritimes line.

But for him, too, this is the end of his personal Long March. The hours on horseback beneath the rain, advancing at walking pace. The sketching of mountain ranges. The smell of dung and wet leather. Meat over the campfire and the sound of barking dogs as they approach villages. He does not know it yet, but never again will he lead explorations. A telegram from Calmette awaits him at the governor general's house, telling him that other telegrams await him in Saigon. Roux and Pasteur want him to proceed to Hong Kong with all possible speed. The big story there is an outbreak of plague. Yersin closes his last explorer's notebook, the ink still fresh and slightly wet.

The elderly, tremulous, freckled hand with the split thumb closes the last explorer's notebook, the ink now dry and faded. The style, too, is dated. Slightly Vidal de la Blache. Spectacles grace Yersin's watery-blue gaze. He is back in Nha Trang once more. The time: summer '40. Closeted in the large, square, arcaded house that has replaced the wooden shack. The enormous, rational cube. The three times one hundred square metres stacked one above the other with the staircase leading to the roof terrace and astronomical observatory. Dr Nam is seventy-seven. For the two months since his return from Europe aboard the little white whale he has been rereading his notebooks. In chronological order. Being whisked back, it seems, to life in the jungle or among the Sedang. Nowadays his legs will no longer support him. It is night. He sits in his rocking chair on the veranda, facing the vast sea that shall soothe all our toiling.

For the last two months, reading those old notebooks has distracted him from History. The passage about the fight with Thouk arouses the memory of that flash of pain, the long wait for death as he lies beneath the trees, watching the play of flame among foliage. He remembers opening his shirt to study the wound, to convince himself that the whole episode did actually happen to him. He no longer feels he has either the strength or the inclination to write his memoirs. He alone, for all time, will know these things, harbour the memory of them.

But no matter. More than anything he ever published, it is the vast correspondence with Fanny and Émilie that tells us the story of his life. Neither woman mislaid a single letter. All of them were found after his sister's death, stuffed into the drawers of a desk. Letters written at one go with no crossings-out and signed either *Yersin*, without his father's first name, or sometimes, ironically, *Dr Nam*. But today, in this summer of '40, unaware of these things, Yersin thinks his life will vanish without trace. Each evening he listens to the world's radio stations on short wave. Summer '40, and the whole world collapsing.

The Vichy government appoints Admiral Decoux, commander of France's Far Eastern Fleet, to the post of governor general of Indochina. Here, as in the mother country, listening to British radio is prohibited. This comes to bother Yersin. He is aware that young men responded to the appeal launched back in June by that peculiar, two-metre-tall general who before the war had been a guest at the Lutetia. He listens to German stations broadcasting propaganda and hailing victory. Once again, war with Germany, and once again Germany will meet defeat following millions of casualties – just as the clairvoyant Rimbaud, then fifteen, predicted after Sedan and the fall of the Second Empire. The Nazis should have read the young prophet when he wrote: 'A government of iron and insanity will make a barracks of all German society, all German thought, only to be smashed in the end by a coalition!'

Five days after the general's appeal from London, the dictator in black and grey who does a fair imitation of Chaplin lands at Le Bourget. It is a Sunday, at five in the morning. The Führer's trip was planned even before the assault, which is why Goering's Stukas spared the Le Bourget runway, enabling the little white whale that would be Air France's last flight to take off. On the wireless, the German commentator describes enthusiastically how the three Mercedes convertibles leave for Paris in the soft light of a June dawn, with a horde of photographers and film-makers in tow. The dictator in black and grey is accompanied by his architect, Albert Speer. He wants to make Berlin an even finer achievement than Paris. They do a lightning tour of the Opéra, La

Madeleine Church, the place de la Concorde, the Champs-Élysées, the Eiffel Tower, the Trocadéro Palace. He is seeing Paris for the first time, the man who in *Mein Kampf* trumpeted his talent for painting, 'surpassed only by my gift for design, particularly in the field of architecture'.

Such self-congratulation is not going to reconcile Yersin with the arts – painting and literature and all that crap. As if the two of them, Hitler and Goering, were waging their world war with the sole aim of expanding their collections and arguing about who should have which Old Master. Yersin wonders what would have become of the young Louis Pasteur if, rather than chemistry, he had taken up portraiture as he planned to do in his distant Jura youth. Pasteur the artist, who in the midst of his scientific research went on teaching at the School of Fine Arts in Paris.

When in that summer of '40, shortly after Yersin last left the Institute, the first Germans present themselves there, they demand to be shown the crypt where Pasteur's body lies. The elderly porter, Joseph Meister, the first man saved from rabies, refuses them entry. The escort jostles him, shoves him aside. The officers descend to the crypt. The old man from Alsace commits suicide in his lodge, using the pistol he brought back from the '14–'18 war.

Yersin learns from a German radio station that the Swastika now flies from the roof terrace of the Lutetia, right above his corner room on the sixth floor. The hotel has been taken over by the Abwehr, the espionage service of the German army. Sitting around the piano, the officers in black and grey are drinking the brandy stocks dry. The Battle of France is followed by the battle for a Britain blitzed by planes sent in by Goering, that other art collector who, without Hitler's knowledge, redirects the occasional aircrew to newly occupied towns and cities to load up works that his own teams of art historians have already located.

Two months after Hitler's visit to Paris, on 20 August Trotsky is assassinated in his Mexican hideout by men sent by Stalin, now allied to Hitler who is himself allied to the Japanese. All the pieces of a global jigsaw are in place. And ten days later, on 30 August, Japanese troops disembark in Tonkin, occupying Haiphong and Hanoi. Laying their swords on the low tables of the Metropole Hotel, the officers set about drinking its brandy stocks dry. Indochina has been invaded. Sitting in his rocking chair facing the sea, Yersin expects the officers of the Kampetai to move into his house any day now, turning the large square building into their Nha Trang command headquarters. There they will search for a bottle of brandy in vain.

They go back a long way, Yersin's run-ins with the Japanese.

Hong Kong

The old man, closing the old notebook, sees himself back in Hanoi, still wearing his explorer's outfit after his descent from Sedang territory, the green canvas jacket and the gear slings for the instruments. Saying goodbye to Father Guerlach. He is thirty-one years old. He goes back down to Saigon and reads the telegram from Roux, whom he has not seen since giving that lecture at the Geographical Society in Paris. The telegrams. Because they tend to fulminate, Roux and Pasteur. They rather bombard authorities with their missives. The Pasteurians still, at that time, see Yersin as one of their own, someone they are holding in reserve for science. Through couriers dispatched to Nha Trang they have learnt that Yersin is away in the mountains. The mountains, mutters Roux with a shrug of irritation.

As if the sea wasn't bad enough.

This is twenty years before the First World War, but already the scientific battle is a political one as well, with the alliances the same. A plague epidemic in China, creeping closer to Tonkin, reaches Hong Kong in May. The Grim Reaper looms on the horizon, and straight away it's carnage. Panic spreads among the British in Kowloon and the French in Haiphong – in every port maintaining trade links with China.

In an earlier age, when people used to walk everywhere, horses worked the land, bullocks drew carts with creaking wheels and ships sailed under canvas, plague advanced at a gentle pace but mowed down all before it nonetheless. Twenty-five million dead in fourteenth-century Europe. Doctors in gowns wore masks with long beaks stuffed full of aromatic herbs to filter foul air. The terror is proportional to the means of transport available: plague bides its time, await-ing steam, electricity, the railway, iron-hulled ocean liners. When the towering figure of the Reaper next brings the black terror, this is no scythe with its rattling hiss through the stalks, this is the crackling roar of the combine harvester, driving through the wheat at full tilt. No cure. Plague is unpredictably fatal, irrationally contagious. It sows ugliness and death, spilling over all the earth the black or yellow pus

of the buboes that burst through victims' skin. The medical
descriptions of the day can be found in the treatise on infectious diseases published by Professor Griesinger of Berlin
University, which quotes Mollaret's book of fifteen years earlier with its mention that plague occurs among 'populations
living in destitution, ignorance, filth, and barbarism to a
degree scarce credible'.

In Saigon, Yersin borrows a certain amount of medical equipment that is then packed carefully into a cabin trunk: test
tubes, coverglasses and an autoclave for sterilising them.
Returning to Hanoi, he meets up with Dr Lefèvre, a Pavie
Mission medic, who is to accompany the explorer of Laos as
far as Muang Sing to delimit the Chinese frontier. Lefèvre is
a politician, and quite frankly, dear colleague, things are
never going to be simple with the British. From Bombay to
Hong Kong the British Raj would occupy one vast uninterrupted territory, but for the intolerable thorn in its flank of
French Indochina. Which is why the British are now turning
for medical assistance to the Japanese (read: the Germans),
playing the Robert Koch Institute off against the Pasteur
Institute.

However, Lefèvre adds, a Francophile Italian, Father
Vigano, an honourable correspondent and former artillery
officer decorated at the Battle of Solferino before entering
holy orders (a Catholic mole among Protestants, says Lefèvre

with a smile), is prepared to stand bail for the Third Republic
as a mark of his gratitude to the Second Empire for bringing
Italy together. To Yersin it makes even less sense than the life
of the Moi. A Swiss and a Wop roped in to help France.
Reaching Hong Kong in mid-June, Yersin makes his way to
the Kennedy Town Hospital run by Dr Lawson.

From the moment of his disembarkation in torrential
rain, Yersin sees the bodies of plague victims lying in the
street, in pools of standing water, in parks, aboard moored
junks. British soldiers, acting on authority, remove the sick
and empty their houses, pile everything up and set fire to it.
They strew lime, pour sulphuric acid, erect red-brick walls
to bar access to infected areas. Yersin takes photographs
and in the evening records his first visions of hell beneath
grey skies and heavy downpours. The flooded hospitals are
resorted to in vain. Wherever he can, in a former glass-
works, in the new abattoir still under construction, in
requisitioned straw huts, Lawson opens lazarets that rapidly
become mortuaries. Mats are thrown down on bare soil and
subsequently burnt with their occupants. Death supervenes
in days. Through curtains of warm rain and squally showers, carts piled high with corpses move at walking pace. 'I
notice many dead rats lying on the ground.' The first note
scribbled by Yersin that evening concerns sewers spewing
out decomposed bodies of rats. Since Camus, that has
seemed obvious, but not then. This is the debt that Camus

owed Yersin when, a mere four years after the latter's death, he wrote his novel.

By telegram, and as a concession to diplomacy, British governor Sir Willliam Robinson gives Yersin explicit authority to come and study plague in Hong Kong. However, bad faith on the British side is clear to see, and it is even worse with the Japanese team under Shibasaburo Kitasato, who intends to reserve all autopsies for himself. Kitasato and his assistant Aoyama are both ex-students of the Koch course. Indeed, Kitasato and Yersin moved to Germany in the same year – Yersin to Marburg and Kitasato to Berlin, where he remained for seven years, staying close to the discoverer of the tuberculosis bacillus. Yet when Dr Lawson re-introduces Yersin to Kitasato, on Yersin's addressing him and his assistant in German, they laugh without answering. 'It seems that, since my time in Germany, I have forgotten the language somewhat, because instead of giving me a reply they enjoyed a private joke.'

Kitasato cannot have been ignorant of Yersin's name and of the fact that he and Roux discovered the diphtheria toxin together. But Kitasato and his lama Koch feel nothing but hostility towards Pasteur and his Institutes. There is also the fact that, in this duel, everyone knows what is at stake. This time the microbe behind bubonic plague, if it is a microbe, is going to be discovered. No longer can it skulk in hiding.

Never again, in the history of humanity, will there be such an opportunity to become the person who vanquished plague. A few more weeks of devastation will mean a few thousand more bodies to study. The microbe's only chance lies in an abrupt, inexplicable halt to the epidemic. Yersin and Kitasato are well aware of owing their presence here to Koch and Pasteur, the two total geniuses of microbiology – Galileos, both of them. They are very conscious of being dwarfs perched on the shoulders of giants. Kitasato, though, has a handicap advantage. Not a single cadaver will be placed at Yersin's disposal.

He might have admitted defeat and set sail for home. But Father Vigano is a dab hand at those borderline-deceitful, Jesuitical methods of which a strict Vaudois Protestant would normally disapprove. For Yersin's benefit he arranges, in just two days, to have a bamboo-framed, straw-covered hut erected near the Alice Memorial Hospital. With the matter of his living-quarters and laboratory settled, Yersin installs a camp bed, unlocks the cabin trunk, and sets out microscope and test tubes. Vigano then greases the palms of the British sailors in charge of the hospital mortuary, where the bodies are stacked prior to being cremated or buried, and buys several from them. Yersin proceeds to ply his scalpel. 'They are already in coffins, covered with lime. I remove some of the lime to expose the crural region.' Yersin is back in Paris, rediscovering the joys of dissection, filling test tubes, doing practical work. 'The bubo is quite distinct. In less than a minute I have it out and take it up to my laboratory. I make a quick preparation and place it under the microscope. One glance reveals a veritable mess of microbes, all similar. They are small stubby rods with rounded ends.'

Enough said. No need to rabbit on interminably. Yersin becomes the first human being to observe the plague bacillus, as Pasteur was the first to observe those of silkworm pebrine, ovine anthrax, chicken cholera and canine rabies. In a week Yersin has penned an article that appears in the September issue of *Annals of the Pasteur Institute*.

What Kitasato describes, having sampled organs and blood and disregarded the bubo, is the pneumococcus of a collateral infection, which he mistakes for the plague bacillus. Without luck, without chance, genius is nothing. The agnostic Yersin is blessed by the gods. Subsequent studies will show that one reason for Kitasato's failure is that he enjoyed the benefits of a proper hospital laboratory, including an incubator set at the temperature of the human body, a temperature at which pneumococcus proliferates, whereas the plague bacillus develops best at approximately twenty-eight degrees centigrade, the mean temperature in Hong Kong at that time of year and the temperature at which Yersin, with no incubator, conducts his observations.

At the same time as sending his results off to Paris, he gives them to Lawson, who loses no time in passing them on to the Japanese. Yersin complains but hardly hits the roof. 'Lawson should have been more discreet. It was he who, having seen my preparations, advised the Japanese to look for the microbe in the bubo. He assured me in person, as did several other people, that the microbe first isolated by the Japanese looked nothing like mine.' Kitasato claims success for himself and kicks off the scientific and political polemic. But proof is later provided and Yersin, who never knew a father and never became a father, at least has paternity attributed to him when his discovery is officially named:

Yersinia pestis.

He shuts himself in his straw hut for a further two months, poring over dead rats and establishing their role in spreading the epidemic. Following the example of Pasteur in France when combing the Beauce region for ovine anthrax, Yersin takes soil samples in the contaminated Tai Ping Shan district and describes them for Calmette's benefit. 'As you know, searching for microbes in soil is not easy. Even if you fail to find one, you cannot conclude that none are present. So it was with an inner conviction that I should find nothing that I undertook this experiment.' He makes preparations of dilute black earth and seeds tubes of gelose containing lengths of platinum wire. 'And lo and behold, in both tubes I obtained several colonies of plague and no other foreign microbe.'

The British now try to retain him as a health officer. The Japanese have gone. Granted, brick walls at the ends of streets may well have kept the Chinese out, but they are likely to have let bugs through. Yersin, however, decides to leave Hong Kong. He writes to the governor general in Hanoi: 'I feel the aim of my mission to Hong Kong has been achieved in that I managed to isolate the plague germ, do the initial work on its physiological properties, and send Paris enough material to work on.' In mid-August he bids a quayside farewell to the good soldier-monk Vigano and takes ship for Saigon, where he writes up his mission report as if on return from an exploration and gives back the borrowed equipment. He records his conclusions in a notebook: 'So plague is a contagious inoculable disease. Probably rats are the main carriers of the disease, but I also ascertained that flies can pass it on.'

In two months in Hong Kong the epic history of bubonic plague is finally tied up. He's on to the next thing. Always in a hurry, Yersin. As if he had identified the bacillus to please the Pasteurian crowd: there you are, in two shakes of a lamb's tail, now I have better things to do, you finish the job. And without a moment's hesitation, in order to speed up development of a vaccine, he puts about samples of his bacillus in sealed glass phials on an almost random basis, writing to Calmette: 'I believe implicitly that you and Mr Roux will have a result before long.'

That is it so far as he is concerned, no more expeditions, no more going to sea. He resolves to make Nha Trang his base, breed sheep, perhaps throw himself into agriculture, opt for real life, take the rough with the smooth. Not for him, ever again, the boring life of the sailor, and he is too old now for exploring or taking on bandits. Also, he has recovered his taste for research, for test tubes and microscopes, practical work. For that, he must raise funds, beg a few pence, cash in on his fame a bit with the authorities. Possibly to alarm them he quotes Molière and La Flèche's muttered aside:

'Plague take all misers and all miserly ways!'

Nha Trang

As soon as he gets back, he sets about installing a modest study centre for epizootic diseases, devising the buildings and breeding programmes himself. A government department gives him a five-thousand-piastre grant. He uses it to fit out a small veterinary laboratory, meaning to conduct research alone and at his own pace. The first lab is hard by the wooden shack at Fishermen's Point, Xom Con, near the sandy beach and the rustling coconut palms beside the jetty where fishermen, gutting their catch at the water's edge each morning, swing machetes to split open the big blue fish and reveal magenta flesh.

He is ready to cease keeping on the move, is Yersin, even

keen to stay put as he stoops over bamboo hutches to feed his experimental menagerie, mice and guinea pigs and monkeys and rabbits. There is no room for buffalo and other bovids here. It's too close to the sea. In the rainy season, when the palm trees have a tousled look, the point sometimes floods. Yersin wants safer ground to build cowsheds and stables. No roads lead into the interior. He canoes up the River Cai, which flows into the sea at this point, and acquires, some dozen kilometres away, the ancient citadel of Khanh Hoa, where he installs about twenty horses and as many cattle and buffalo. He needs a vet.

In Nha Trang, Yersin recruits fishermen's sons, turning them into lab assistants to help him run his little establishment. Through Calmette he buys equipment, glassware in the main, which is carefully unloaded from the *Saigon* when it calls in and brought ashore in small boats, along with scientific journals and the new Peugeot bicycle he has ordered from that ingenious French craftsman. He spends his mornings on the terrace, drawing up plans. In the afternoon he supervises building work on the laboratory. Come evening, he shuts himself in his shack, penning his book, *With the Moi*, of which he will have fifteen copies printed at his own expense. Yersin never seeks honours, but neither does he ever turn them down. On Calmette's advice he hires an army vet, Pesas, who joins him from Saigon and will soon number among the fallen on microbiology's field of honour.

He hopes to settle here, Yersin – here at Fishermen's Point, looking out over the sparkling waters of the bay and the clumps of areca where the betel creeper twines, the coconut palms, the children, the nets that the womenfolk darn on the beach and, when evening comes, the flying of bats, far from the epileptic frenzy of towns and cities, surrounded by real existence. Sometimes, at night, he recalls Captain Flotte, to whom he ultimately owes all this – Nha Trang, the exploring, the fame. 'Though bits of ribbon are in general of supreme indifference to me, I am very pleased to have been awarded the Legion of Honour because that is going to make many things easier for me.' Here too, as with demography and life expectancy, we must scrupulously avoid anachronism. The ribbon is not, at that time, given to footballers.

That year a young cavalry officer, Hubert Lyautey (who comes from two years in Algeria, where he said one or two critical things about the colonial system), an heir of the little Saharian crowd and of Captain Rimbaud, calls on Yersin in his retreat. Their meeting in the scientist's wooden shack is recorded by Noël Bernard, Yersin's first biographer. The two men are cut from the same cloth.

Lyautey, returning from a mission to Madagascar, admires the spirit of enterprise shown by this Pasteurian who discovered the plague bacillus, a man who might shine in the salons of Paris. He visits the cattle sheds, the stables and the little laboratory at the water's edge. 'Starting out with no natural resources, he nevertheless acquired, for fifteen piastres apiece, twenty horses as inoculation animals, took on a vet named Pesas whom he trained and filled with enthusiasm – and was launched. Moreover, one derives great solace from hours spent in this still-rudimentary establishment, where a young scientist without personal needs or requirements is entirely caught up in his work.'

For the past few months, the talk of Paris has been the Dreyfus Affair. As once, centuries before, Jews were blamed for spreading plague, they are now suspected of fomenting defeat and betraying the French nation. Yersin regrets having so little news. 'You ask what I think of the Dreyfus Affair, but I cannot know what I think when no one has the details of the case. In all probability, if the generals refuse to divulge them it is because doing so would cause grave inconvenience.'

Lyautey is one of those who have assumed the captain's innocence from the outset. He has risked putting his doubts about the court martial's ruling in writing. 'What increases our scepticism is that we think we see in it pressure from what they call opinion, namely public opinion, what the man in the street thinks.' And both men despise public opinion, the vulgar thinking of the mob. 'The mob yells "Death to the Jew!" because Dreyfus is Jewish and nowadays anti-Semitism is all the rage.' But here is a gay sticking up for a yid. The blind man and the lame. It is to lead to an involuntary coming-out and to what was said of him by Clemenceau, albeit a Dreyfusard himself, when he feigns admiration for Lyautey's courage: 'Here is an admirable man, a brave man, one who has always had balls between his legs, even if in addition to his own.' French political life is still, at the time, a very male thing, and debates in the Chamber often culminate in pistols at dawn. Yersin is well aware that, whatever he does, he is not going to find it easy to keep his distance from all the filth of politics.

Madagascar

Ce n'est pas une vie que de ne pas bouger.

He was twenty-six years old when, at the end of a letter to Fanny written from Paris, he penned this Rimbaldian alexandrine: 'It is no way to live, not keeping on the move.' He has kept on the move quite a lot. Now thirty-two, he is once more handed a telegram when the *Saigon* calls in. Unfolding the sheet of blue paper in his wooden shack, Yersin may be starting to curse the invention. He is asked to 'leave as soon as possible for Diego-Suarez to study the bilious fever microbe'. The Republic is dispatching him on a mission, and he leaves Nha Trang for Saigon by steamship.

His financial situation has improved. He wears an off-white suit of excellent cut and takes with him a young man whose functions are clear if difficult to pinpoint. Is he lab assistant, secretary, or personal aide? From this time on, Yersin is accompanied on all trips by, turn and turn about, one of the small group of what he terms 'my Annamite servants', his own little crowd, fishermen's sons whom he has turned into laboratory technicians but also mechanics for the machines and soon for the cars and lorries. In front of the Arsenal, the two men board the Messageries Maritimes ship bound for Aden on the first leg of their journey.

This time Yersin goes ashore in Yemen, where the French consul gives him the ministry's instructions. He discovers the hellish cauldron on the edge of the great erg, the vitrifying sun of Rub' al-Khali and Arabia Petraea: 'All around is completely arid sandy desert. Here, however, the walls of the crater keep the air out and we roast at the bottom of this hole as if in a limekiln.' The Whites receive him in his white suit like a star, a harbinger of modernity, picking up his tabs on the terrace of the Grand Hôtel de l'Univers at Steamer Point, not far from the house belonging to a merchant named Bardey where the poet acquired such wealth, the poet who had died four years before but was still much talked of in this place for the eight kilos of gold around his waist that distorted his gait. Surely Yersin will never be as rich as Rimbaud.

After Arabia comes Africa, and the two men take their

time. The servant, one imagines, is not disappointed with the trip. They are Fix and Phileas Fogg. Very posh. Yersin visits Egypt and goes off to see the pyramids and the temples, takes a felucca and travels up the green waters of the Nile, aware that Livingstone died in Tanganyika while trying to find the source of the river there. He embarks for Zanzibar, then Réunion, where he stays for a while, finding out about agriculture, flowers, and cinnamon, and here Baudelaire's lines precede him:

> …'neath the unseen aegis of an angel
> The deprived child soaks up intoxicating sun.

There follows a slow descent of the Indian Ocean, a crossing of the line, the ship slides through gold and shimmering ripples, the Mozambique Channel, the Comoros Islands, Madagascar. After three months of roaming, the two choose to settle on Nossi-Bé. They reside on the island 'rather than go to Majunga because Majunga no more has bilious fever than Nossi-Bé has and Nossi-Bé is an infinitely more pleasant place to live'. Yersin loves seaside locations.

Sitting in a rocking chair on a shaded veranda, quenching his thirst with sips from a glass of cold water from the Chamberland filter, or possibly lemonade, he savours existence in a country that has neither winter nor summer, where life is one perpetual, verdant spring, unconstrained, wholly gratuitous. He is sure that his mission is gratuitous too, but he follows instructions, travels about a bit, takes samples, prepares microscope and syringes, studies the vegetation and arboriculture, discovers curious trees and luscious fruit. It is his first encounter with *Hevea brasiliensis*, a rubber tree.

Rolling a sticky ball of latex between the palms of his hands, Yersin pokes it with a finger, stretches it out, moulds it into a ring: a tyre for his Peugeot bicycle. He marvels at the intuition and genius of the inventor of the rubber tyre. He conjectures that the name Dunlop will remain more firmly lodged in human memory than that of the man who discovered the plague bacillus. Because plague will die out and tyres will proliferate. It may, though, have been beyond his powers of conjecture to foresee that in a hundred years' time machines with tyres – bicycles, then cars, motorbikes, lorries, planes – would inflict quite as much mayhem as the Black Death.

His Madagascar mission has more to do with politics than science, and Yersin is not deceived. This is all about colonisation. It is the image of France that he has been sent there to promote, as Lyautey will be asked to promote it in Morocco. In the cells at police headquarters, bad cop and good cop take turns. If the presence of Yersin fails to persuade the Malagasy, Gallieni will be sent in.

And since the Malagasy play up, Gallieni is sent in.

the vaccine

As for Yersin, that summer he is recalled. This is five years after his leaving Paris. One year after his stay in Hong Kong and the famous discovery. The government of the Republic demands that he return to the Pasteur Institute and deal with his damned bacillus. The authorities are beginning to have nightmares about plague germs dormant in glass vials in the middle of Paris. Because for all that people have been cultivating and fussing over his wretched bacillus for a year now, not much progress has been made. In fact, they are going round in circles. Why go on raising, in fragile glass phials, generation after generation of a bacteriological bomb that might well – through a lab assistant's clumsiness, say, or deliberate action by some unhinged agent, a researcher in a foul mood, cuckolded possibly, or a Japanese or German terrorist commando – launch a fresh outbreak of bubonic plague and revive the Black Death in the fifteenth arrondissement, wiping out the entire population of the capital?

Yersin moves into the Institute because the Lutetia has yet to be built. What's taking them so long, the Boucicaut family? 'I am putting up at the Pasteur Institute again. I am very pleased about this because it means I can do my job more easily, and besides the place is so familiar!' He sets to work, together with Roux and Calmette, promising Fanny that he will pop in and see her at Fig Tree House one of these days.

The lion tamer has been sent for, and he arrives at rue Dutot to find his beast anaemic, on the verge of depression, sitting around in pyjamas all day, unshaven, chain-smoking. 'I must restore my microbe to his former virulence, he's been a bit neglected in my absence. Then I shall seed a large number of balloon-flasks of soup to make the toxin. While that is forming in the incubator I hope to be able to put in a brief appearance at Morges.' The little chintz parlour will not accommodate all the press. Yersin is now world news.

It is warm inside a chicken, as everyone knows. Forty-two degrees. Far warmer than inside a sheep. Even with its woolly jumper on.

Pasteur is the first to slide thermometers up virtually every orifice, cloaca or anus, discovering that the high temperatures of certain birds prevent viruses from developing inside them. If you inoculate a hen with ovine anthrax she couldn't give a damn, she laughs it off. The bug tickles, at worst. But plunge the bird into a bath of cold water and she starts to look less clever, the virus eventually kills her off. Take the drenched hen out in time and despite being infected she will recover unaided, flapping her wings to warm herself up and squawking insults at the researcher. Yersin progresses to pigeons.

The pigeon is a kind of flying rat, with wings screwed on and a coat of grey paint applied. A feathered creature that nevertheless spends most of its time on the ground and is frequently lame, hobbling along on stumps like a leper without a crutch. However, there is one big difference: the bird, unlike the rodent, has a natural immunity to plague.

Yersin lines up the whole rue Dutot menagerie, from the smallest to the largest. From Molière he passes to La Fontaine and animals struck by plague, then to the Grimms' fairy tale of the animal musicians standing on one another's shoulders on their way to Bremen, the donkey at the bottom and the rooster on top. He tries to reduce the bug's virulence in order to obtain on the one hand a vaccine and on the other an anti-plague serum. For two months, quite as if it is the easiest thing in the world and we need only run a film of him, speeded up, he works at his bench, juggles equipment, takes samples, lights burners, goes for a pee, washes his hands, performs injections, scribbles notes. A white-coated Yersin bustling about and the laboratory animals that, though increasing in size, are clearly not happy about being stabbed with larger and larger syringes. The tamer's whip cracks in mid-ring as each poor beast clambers onto its stool, tendering its bum for the jab.

At each stage, a rattling drum roll and Charleston-esque cymbal clash from the orchestra: Yersin immunising a mouse! Yersin immunising a guinea pig! Yersin immunising a rabbit! Yersin immunising a horse! Yersin has no elephant available. A slap on the horse's rump, take him away, he slips out a fountain pen, unscrews the cap, composes a rundown, Calmette assisting, for the house journal, the *Annals of the Pasteur Institute*, 'Bubonic plague, note two': 'These serother-apeutic experiments are therefore worth pursuing. If the results obtained with animals continue to be satisfactory, it will be time to try applying the same method to the preven-tion and treatment of plague in man.' He screws the cap back on, removes his white coat, hands the sheet to Roux, and that's it: he announces his departure, I'll leave you to wash up. When Roux presents the vaccine against plague to old man Pasteur, now impotent but still dolled up in his black frockcoat and bow tie, the two men, looking up from the microscope, feel vindicated, fully aware that, were Yersin to approach them for a reference for building a moon rocket, they would borrow his pen and unscrew the cap.

Yersin, already impatient to get back to sea, nevertheless makes numerous calls before leaving Paris, contacting the Foreign Ministry, the Ministry of the Colonies, and the Geographical Society. He wants to set up a laboratory at Nha Trang that can prepare large quantities of the serum, where he will be able to continue his experiments on monkeys before passing to man. 'I meet with a degree of rivalry, which leaves me supremely indifferent.'

By early August he is aboard the *Melbourne*, steaming east at sixteen knots. That is a record, as Yersin duly notes. During this voyage from Marseilles to Saigon he keeps a close eye on the phials of bacilli that his Messageries colleague keeps for him in the pharmacy. Back in Paris, where the government ministers now sleep like babes, the horse remedy is found. That September, Pasteur dies. He receives a state funeral. His delight is to be leaving his Institute in the hands of a 'crowd', as it were, a band of young men who for years have served as his eyes as well as his arms and legs and who will continue the great work when he is gone. Roux and Calmette will still be at the helm nearly forty years later.

Yersin is also taking with him a new type of camera, the Photo-Jumelle, an ingenious system of folding viewfinders that exploits parallax to make prints appear to be in relief.

He takes pictures at each port of call. On his return he is to publish an article on it in a Hanoi journal, the *Illustrated Indochina Review*.

In Colombo he buys a pair of mongooses.

Canton

Before the Chinese, who think they can do anything, took the liberty of giving their cities, even their capital, Chinese names, any old civvy used to be able to find his way around without opening an atlas. It is at Guangzhou, then, that Yersin disembarks. Guangzhou is already, at that time, a city of nearly two million inhabitants. The plague epidemic has just killed a hundred and fifty thousand of them. Yersin has brought some of the Paris vaccine with him and, from Nha Trang, the horse vaccine developed by his vet Pesas. Intending to apply the horse remedy to the Chinese and looking for his own Joseph Meister, he bumps into the French consul in Canton-Guangzhou. He does not conceal from the man that only up to the horse stage has his vaccine been shown to be harmless.

The consul scratches his head. The thing is: the Chinese have long memories. It may be thirty-five years since France and Britain sacked the Summer Palace and the same length of time since the two nations, by winning the Second Opium War, forced the Chinese to open their ports to the drug trade. The fact remains: neither the French nor the British are exactly welcome, being confined to particular quarters. It will be in poor taste for some syringe-wielding long-nose to turn up and euthanise a few invalids. Still scratching his head, the consul congratulates Yersin on his discovery – as well as on his fame, which has reached even these parts – but warns him that he risks a serious case of cold shoulder, or rather reminds him that, as they used to say in the diplomatic service, the Tarpeian Rock lies not far from the Capitol.

Had he been Catholic, Yersin would have become a saint, the conqueror of bubonic plague would have been canonised on the spot, so undeniably does the story seem supernaturally inspired. Moreover it rests, that story, on three testimonies that tally independently: Yersin's own, kept at the Pasteur Institute; the bishop's, no doubt to be found in the archives of the Holy See; and that of the consul in the equivalent quai d'Orsay facility.

The diplomat sends his report over the next few days:

On Friday, 26 June, around 11 a.m., I received a visit from Dr Yersin, who after explaining the object of his mission asked me whether I thought he would be successful in obtaining entry to the Chinese plague hospitals and there conducting trials of the curative serum he had discovered. In my reply to the doctor I made no secret of the fact that I could not possibly authorise him to attempt in this place the experiments he wished to carry out, experiments that the hostility of the Cantonese population to all things European might make extremely dangerous for Residents. I suggested to the doctor that, before leaving Canton, he should accompany me to the Catholic mission.

The two are received there by His Grace, Bishop Chausse, who as it happens is about to call a doctor anyway. He is concerned for the health of a young seminarian of eighteen, Tisé by name, who has been complaining for the past few days of headaches and a violent pain in the groin. The young man's temperature having soared that morning, he is now in bed. This troubles His Grace, particularly since converts are hardly plentiful, and with God taking this one ... well, what sense does that make? Tisé has just been given Extreme Unction. He has become convinced, this young Chinese, that over the centuries since Jesuits started evangelising in these parts there has been plenty of time for a Chinatown to become established in the Garden of Eden, complete with bilingual tea-houses signposted in Mandarin and Latin. Prayers are being said at his bedside in expectation of his sprouting gorgeous white wings.

Yersin: 'Bishop Chausse takes me to the patient at 3 p.m.: the young Chinese is drowsy, he cannot stand without vertigo, he is in a state of extreme lassitude, his temperature is raised, his tongue furred. The right groin shows a thickening very painful to the touch. We are looking at a confirmed case of bubonic plague, and the violence of the initial symptoms means it can be classed as serious.'

The consul: 'I make no objection to the anti-plague serum inoculation being administered, merely insisting that this be done with no other Chinese present and with the details being kept strictly secret until the invalid's full recovery. That way we can avoid any bother that might occur should the intervention fail.'

Yersin: 'At five o'clock, six hours after the onset of the disease, I inject 10 cc of serum. At the time the invalid is vomiting and raving, both very alarming signs of the rapid advance of the infection. At 6 and 9 p.m., further injections of 10 cc apiece. Between 9 p.m. and midnight, no change, the invalid remaining drowsy, restless, complaining frequently. His temperature remains very high and he has some diarrhoea. From midnight the invalid becomes calmer, and at 6 a.m., just as Father Director arrives to find out how the plague victim is doing, the young man wakes up and says he feels better. His temperature has indeed dropped to normal. The lassitude and other serious symptoms are gone. The groin area is no longer painful to the touch, and the thickening has virtually disappeared. The cure is so rapid that, had not several persons besides myself seen the patient the previous day, I should be inclined to doubt whether this was a true case of plague. Understandably, that night spent at the bedside of my first plague victim is one of intense worry. In the morning, however, when dawn brings success, all is forgotten, even my tiredness.'

Yersin becomes the first doctor to save a victim of bubonic plague.

The consul and the bishop each undertake to bear witness to the extraordinary event. Well-nigh miraculous, murmurs the bishop, whose word is to be believed. The Lord does indeed move in ways so mysterious that a Swiss Prot will on occasion snatch a Chink Holy Joe from the jaws of death.

However, there was to be no St Yersin whose relic – a toe, possibly, or a kneecap – would bring processions of devout pilgrims to Morges. It would be nice, of course, to hear what became of the young seminarian, have news of him, write a *Life of Tisé*, the first man cured of plague. Did he enter a Catholic monastery? Did he, like Joseph Meister, commit suicide when the Japanese invaded? We shall never know.

The consul advises Yersin to leave Canton for Amoy, or in

today's parlance Guangzhou for Xiamen, a small port boasting a field hospital for seamen that lies opposite Formosa, now called Taiwan. Sailors matter not a lot. Ghosts, almost, even then. Remember what Plato said.

The old age of ships is like that of men: one slow decline. Caught up in the excitement of his vaccinations and lacking, unlike us, the time to consult the naval records, packed with romance and coincidence though they are, Yersin doubtless fails to notice, a jetty's length from where he disembarks in Xiamen, the skeleton of the *Volga*, the trusty vessel that once carried him to and fro, with the regularity of clockwork, between Saigon and Manila, since taken out of service and that very year sold for scrap to the China Merchants Co., which in the ship's final days is using it here as a hulk.

As for the *Saigon*, on whose bridge good Captain Flotte had held his exhausted frame upright, she had gone aground, also that year, a typhoon driving her onto the sands of Poulo Condor Island. A stranger to such maritime nostalgia, in the space of a few days Yersin inoculates twenty-three patients with his absolutely modern anti-plague serum, two of whom only, treated too late, succumb despite everything. Afterwards he travels to Portuguese Macau. He is keen to cock a snook at the British, well knowing that word of his victorious vaccinations will cross the bay.

Let them send for their friend Kitasato, who can do nothing.

Bombay

Back in Nha Trang, Yersin immediately asks Pesas to step up production of the vaccine, and Pesas, true to his military background, says he will. Yersin then sails for Marseilles to go and gather his laurels. Accompanied by his lab assistant, he reaches Paris in November, meets up with Roux and Calmette, and the four men go to meditate before the mortal remains of Louis Pasteur, which since his state funeral have lain in a vault at Notre-Dame while the Institute crypt is made ready to receive them. Over several pages of the *Bulletin of the Academy of Medicine* Yersin draws a metaphorical line under the great history of plague. He would have received the Nobel had the Nobel existed. The first one will be awarded five years hence. The prize is unheard-of as yet. Alfred Nobel dies that December, and the provisions are in his will.

After one month at sea and three weeks on land, there they both are on the Marseilles quayside. A life at high speed, a whirlwind existence. Phileas Fogg and his Fix, eyes glued to train and steamship timetables, scuttling up gangplanks, leaping onto railway-carriage steps. How strange that old Verne, who wrote about Livingstone, never devoted a novel to the hectic, incredible adventures of Yersin, portraying him as the kind of positive hero who might inspire moral inflorescence among young readers. When the ship calls at Colombo, a British delegation, possibly mounted on elephants, sweeps into the port with the local maharajah in attendance. A high-ranking officer boards the *Melbourne* and asks to meet Yersin. Plague has reached Bombay.

In his cabin, Yersin has no serum and no vaccination animals. Wait here, I'll be right back. He steps ashore at Nha Trang just as twenty-four mares have died of anthrax. Yersin asks Pesas to get busy on the survivors. 'The moment I arrived we bled the two mares that seem to me best immunised. If their serum is good, I shall take large blood samples and leave for India immediately.'

'Immediately' is in fact a matter of weeks, and there is one boat a month. They produce serum until February. Yersin takes away hundreds of doses in his luggage when he is going to need tens of thousands. Meanwhile, Pesas continues to busy himself – too much, possibly. As with any kind of precision work, the risk lies in routine. He runs from kiln to grinder, dashes from lab to menagerie with crazy haste. The monkeys play pranks, the mares kick up their heels, hooves catch pails, the mongooses tread in their feeding-troughs and tip them over. Yersin is at sea and Pesas falls victim to a lab accident.

The telegram reporting that Pesas has died of an infection arrives at the Colombo office of Messageries Maritimes. Yersin has already left for Tamil Nadu, going on to Madras, from where he crosses the subcontinent by train, heading for Bombay. In March he takes up residence at the French consulate, where he vaccinates the French community, healing the daughter of the manager of the Comptoir d'escompte bank who has already contracted the disease. It is with the British that the trouble starts.

Bombay is a major port with eight hundred thousand inhabitants, and its trade with London is of vital importance. Almost globally, it seems, colonial empires are disputing frontiers, their armies facing off across imaginary lines. This is the 'Great Game' described by Arthur Conolly. The year before, at Muang Sing, the French made the British quit northern Laos, forcing them westward across the Mekong. One year on, the British take revenge at Fashoda, forcing the French from the banks of the Nile. Loti has yet to write *India (Without the British)*. Yersin, one feels, would not have been averse to the idea.

Medical missions from all corners of the earth pounce on the Indian plague victims. Doctors from Russia, Austria, Germany, Egypt, Britain and Italy, all *in situ* before Yersin, fight over the dying and steal medical secrets from one another in an atmosphere of conspiracy and incompetence. The activities of the health authorities are as problematic and incoherent as were those of the Chinese in Hong Kong. Locals refuse to set foot in any isolation hospitals and plague houses that fail to observe the caste system. The place teems with rats, but extermination runs counter to the Buddhist principle of respect for life. Pasteurians themselves are divided over the so-called 'Haffkine's lymph' controversy.

Haffkine, Yersin's successor as teacher of the microbiology course, recently left the Institute to open his own laboratory in Calcutta, where he produces the lymph that others blame for appalling side effects. Dr Bonneau is sent out from Paris. The Inspector-General of Colonial Medicine and his assistants conduct their inquiry. The Bonneau crowd eventually sort out the differences splitting the Pasteur crowd. As the Inspector-General writes in his report: 'Albeit persuaded of the possibility of vaccinating human beings against plague using heated cultures, we condemn the Haffkine procedure as being

---

too summary and too rapid to confer true immunity, and we consider the dangers it poses, compared with the advantages, more than sufficient to justify that condemnation.'

As for Yersin, the confusion is such that his actions are wholly undermined by the deceitful British:

> Dr Yersin encountered numerous difficulties on this score. Taking his cases from hospitals directed by British doctors, he never had the full freedom of action that he needed: iodine injections were made into the buboes presenting on his patients, the latter were prescribed strychnine, belladonna, strophanthin – all ineffective if not harmful drugs – with the result that statistics based on such cases were not as valuable as they might have been had the cases been left to his own initiative.

For Yersin, these disputes are exhausting. He is keenly aware that he must get out, go away, find his own Levant, his own Harar.

He's thoroughly fed up with Bombay and the British. The feeling is mutual. The British have no time for these young Frenchmen who are not French at all or not entirely (Yersin being Swiss by birth and Haffkine originating from Ukraine) but who promptly, once in Paris, pick up what the British find most execrable about the French: that audacious way of talking down to anyone and everyone, particularly the British; that imperial, one can only say 'Pasteurial' attitude.

Yersin leaves Bombay to get away from the medical community. In Mandvi, in the very north of Gujarat, on the Kutch peninsula, where the epidemic is killing a hundred people a day, he is alone. His serum supply soon starts to run low, and he decides enough is enough. He writes to Calmette to say he is off. He already, by this time, has a well-deserved reputation for being something of a grouch, not to say a pain in the neck. It would be nice to know that, at the station, he bought the two volumes of the *Jungle Book*, which Kipling had recently published. Kipling will soon be awarded the Nobel, which Yersin will never receive. Meanwhile, plague has reached Suez.

The Pasteur Institute sends Paul-Louis Simond to Bombay as Yersin's replacement. In a letter to the newcomer, Calmette puts him on his guard: 'Yersin is a good man but, it has to be said, overly uncouth. His attitude in Bombay was most disagreeable, and I fear you may have some difficulty in remedying the unpleasant impression he made there.'

Simond does indeed meet with a cold reception, and the image of the Pasteurians left by Yersin and Haffkine is rather that of a crowd of conceited young men, haughty and cocksure, who tend to respond with a wordless shrug to all offers of advice. Simond complains of this to Paris, and Calmette writes back: 'As regards Yersin, I am not at all surprised by what you tell me. With his uncouth manner he will have behaved very clumsily towards his British colleagues.' It takes Simond a whole year to smooth things over. He does in the end gain acceptance by discovering that it is the flea that carries the epidemic.

Yersin, reading the report back in Nha Trang, shakes his head. Focusing on rats had made him overlook fleas. The flea is a pterygoid insect, as his father must undoubtedly have known. Simond's simple experiment consists in shutting an infected rat in a wire cage and surrounding it with other wire cages containing new rats, as purpose-bred laboratory animals are called. Ever the good sport, Yersin offers Simond his congratulations on having, with this codicil, completed the aetiology of the disease.

He was never one for staying put, either, not Simond. Where is his old friend today, Yersin wonders. This is the early part of '41. Yersin is now seventy-eight years old.

Communications between Europe and Indochina are virtually impossible – random, certainly, being subject to censorship by the Japanese occupier at this end and the German occupier back there. It's getting on for a year since Yersin stepped out of the little white whale, and in his enforced idleness he imagines old friends in the grinder of war. In the large, square-set Nha Trang house he listens to French radio, decoding the ideology of Vichyism, and to

British radio, starting to admire the only nation to offer resistance. German radio, still addressing the gallery, sings the praises of the Molotov–Ribbentrop pact, vaunting the complicity between Nazism and Stalinism, until suddenly, come June, German tanks invade the Soviet Union. Yersin is under no illusion, perhaps telling himself that war is to politics what fornication is to love – a route that must sometimes, just sometimes, be taken. He asks himself: has it really been worth it, growing so old?

Has it really been worth the candle, all this progress that he himself helped to usher in? Already, physicists closeted in Los Alamos are inventing atomic weapons. Elsewhere, discoveries made by Pasteurians are being used to manufacture biological weapons.

Listening to Swiss radio in '41, Yersin learns of the death, in Zurich that January, of the Irish writer who was his neighbour at the Lutetia. Joyce firmly believed that this entire world war was one vast conspiracy against publication of his *Finnegans Wake*, finished at last. All this news comes to him in disorder and confusion. The Thai army, allied to the Japanese, has invaded Cambodia and Laos, destroying the French airport at Angkor where the little white Air France whale stopped off on its way here. A letter from the governor general in Hanoi, Admiral Decoux, tells him of the death of Loir, Pasteur's nephew, reminding him of when the little crowd was still at the rue Vauquelin premises, before Loir's departure for Australia. When last heard of he was in Le Havre. Never a good idea, living in a port during wartime. As for the Gulag and Treblinka, what does Yersin know of them, sitting alone at night by his radio?

He knows that Jews in Paris wear the yellow star. It is ages since he was last in touch with his student friend Sternberg. Is Sternberg an old retired doctor in Marburg these days, avoiding the ban on practising by practising no longer? When he passes Aryans in the street, must he step off the pavement? Recalling their hopes and their conversations about plague, Yersin is reminded of the old French proverb: *Qui veut noyer son chien l'accuse de la rage* – 'Feel like drowning your dog? Say it has rabies.' He knows that at the entrance to square Boucicaut, down below the Lutetia, there is now a sign that reads

Play area
Infants only
No Jews

After Pearl Harbor in December comes the war in the Pacific, with the Americans directing their armada towards the Philippines. Months go by, and the news is consistently bad. It is now '42. Zweig, who like Yersin spends his evenings listening to the radio, commits suicide in Petrópolis on hearing of the fall of Singapore, because all is now lost. Yersin turns seventy-nine.

Admiral Decoux, a refugee in Dalat, is pestering him to rewrite the great history of the Hong Kong plague and the first vaccinations in China. He is well aware that they want to use him for propaganda purposes, to conscript him into their ideological war. To issue a reminder, in this Indochina under Japanese occupation, that the Pasteur Institute triumphed over the Koch Institute back then, with Yersin trumping Kitasato, that it was no Axis scientist who conquered the Great Black Death. Genius is on the side of the Allies.

He has been rereading his notebooks and writing up his exploration souvenirs, so the job is a cinch. It appears in the newspapers. He well knows that, once again, what is being exploited here is his immense prestige – something that is a mere genetic accident, coupled with his being the last survivor of the Pasteur crowd. Certain Vietnamese are plotting with the occupier to eject a defeated France. To counter such ingratitude, Vichy is keen to remind Vietnam that all those roads, those railway lines, those water towers, those hospitals – that was the Japs, was it?

real life

Just like the rest of us, Yersin is looking for happiness.

The difference being that he finds it.

After Bombay, no more medicine. Let plague be relegated to
the corpus of medical science. Yersin, at thirty-five, means to
savour the privilege of withdrawing from politics, opting out
of History. Choosing the sort of serene solitude that fosters
poetic and scientific research. He is in the prime of life. Black
of beard and blue of eye. The right way to live is no longer,
after all, keeping on the move. Being on the move the whole
time is now what bothers him. He has had enough. It is beginning to get on his wick. He has found paradise, it is called

Nha Trang, and he never wants to leave it again. He wants to make it even lovelier, create a Pasteur Institute here, have done with the make-do-and-mend, cottage-industry approach that cost Pesas his life.

Seated at his desk in a cane chair, the scientific journals before him, Yersin studies architecture and turns himself into a builder. Abandoning the wooden shack at Fishermen's Point, he designs a house that is a three-storey brick cube with two-metre-wide arched galleries all around it. On the ground floor: the kitchen. On the first floor: the bedroom. On the top floor: the study and library with its serried ranks of scientific journals. The view from the roof is panoramic, high above a perpetual bedazzlement of beauty, the fishing boats making their way down the river each evening, lighting lamps that hang from long poles, sailing out to sea. And at dawn the wind bringing them home. Men unloading fish and prawns on the beach. Near by, the yard where shipwrights work on the ribs of fresh sampans. The fragrance of flowers and the smell of earth after a rainshower drift up to the study where Yersin has begun designing accommodation for the vets and lab assistants, houses with whitewashed walls and woodwork painted light green, brown-tiled roofs and verandas – the style that of the seaside villas he remembers from Cabourg in Normandy.

On a site set just back from the shore the Institute itself

will stand, a building fifty metres long by ten metres wide, containing laboratories and rooms in which to bleed animals, with lean-tos adjacent for stabling the bullocks and horses currently undergoing immunisation against various diseases. The project has the backing of Yersin's friend Doumer, still governor general, the orphan from Aurillac who founded Dalat. Yersin recruits labourers and grooms, the latter to rear and tend the stock, the former to develop the agriculture that feeds it. 'I am currently building a windmill that will serve to draw water.'

Seated at his desk in a cane chair, the scientific journals before him, Yersin studies physics, mechanics and electricity. He has the Messageries boat bring equipment from Paris, a chest incubator and sterilising oven, a Pictet gas-powered ice-making machine. A water pump and turbine will supply electricity to the Institute as well as to the fishing village. He tries to keep costs down by lending a hand himself, and anyway these are his kites he is building: 'This area of physics has always intrigued me, and I know enough about it to do the installation work myself without needing to call in a specialist electrical engineer.' He writes off to Serpollet, ordering his first steam-powered automobile, a Serpollet 5-CV that can reach speeds up to twenty-five kilometres an hour.

Yersin is crafting a waking dream, bringing it to fruition. Before long he is the owner of a five-hundred-hectare estate at Suoi Giao, now known as Suoi Dau. At the time it is a patch of scrub some twenty kilometres inland. A tributary of the river that flows past his Nha Trang house enables him to access the estate by sampan. The land is cleared, grazing prepared, cereals planted. Yersin is fashioning a miniature, self-sufficient planet, a metonymic world, an ark of salvation, a Garden of Eden from which viruses are banned (they are consigned to hell). The ponds are dragged for weeds. Soon there are hundreds of bullocks, buffalo, horses, cows, three hundred sheep and as many goats. The stock is divided between paddocks containing groups of fifty or more individuals held in isolation, with a guarded double enclosure protecting them from large wild animals and tiny bacilli.

The new task he now assigns himself is that of scientist supreme, multiplier of progressive steps. He is surrounded by sons of fishermen who have become Pasteurians and by existing Pasteurians who have come out from Paris and Saigon. The new laboratories host research into strangles, tetanus, anthrax, surra, foot-and-mouth, pasteurellosis, barbone disease and piroplasmosis. Yersin orders crates of bells from Switzerland, having them shipped out via Marseilles. 'Since our cows have been wearing bells, tigers take fewer of them and now seem to seek out our horses.' And then, just like that, the century silently turns.

The twentieth century opens without anyone knowing that it will be the worst yet, a century of infinite barbarity coming right after one of dreams of infinite progress. However, it begins well enough with the fanfare of the *belle époque*. The world still holds plenty of the optimism of science and technology as well as of diseases eradicated and the prospect of further preventive and curative vaccinations to come.

Seated at his desk in a cane chair, the scientific journals before him, Yersin studies agronomy and chemistry. He runs experiments in substituting paddy for oats in horse feed, he introduces terraced cultivation on hilly ground to outsmart and remould climates. When Arabica fails, two thousand Liberia coffee trees are planted. So are medicinal plants, including a thousand *Erythroxylum coca* plants for the manufacture of cocaine, then widely used in pharmacy.

Following the Indian winter provoked by his mood swings, Yersin's relations with Paris have warmed. 'Dear Calmette, incredible but true: I've received a letter from Roux, postmarked Ceyzérieu! A real stroke of luck for me, because when our friend Roux decides to take up his pen, it is invariably to write interesting things.' He makes the trip to Paris. 'I was going to take the Trans-Siberian, but I fear it may still be too cold at the moment.' Ploughing and pasturage are not among the primary missions of the Pasteur Institute, they are hardly the twin dugs that suckle it. A private company is set up with the names 'Messrs Yersin, Roux and Calmette'.

The exchanges that follow his return to Nha Trang do occasionally, with hindsight, read like the phone records of a cartel. Here is Roux writing to Yersin:

Bertrand's first concern after your departure was to find some tungsten acid. He located some in England, and we ordered a ton at the fantastic price of six thousand five hundred francs. It's not to be had for less. This will be dispatched to Saigon via Hamburg. The sulphuric acid will be shipped through Marseilles, likewise the silicate. As you see, we've decided to take a big risk. There's no indication that, in present circumstances, cocaine will bring in major profits. Particularly since a very serious competitor has just come on the market in the shape of a new substance prepared synthetically, stovaine, which is a less toxic anaesthetic than cocaine and just as effective at double dose.

Oddly, the letter makes no mention of the fact that the man who invented stovaine only months before is himself a Pasteurian from the Institute, Ernest Fourneau, a chemist like Pasteur.

Yersin develops his production, concocting a liquid concentrate that might have made him the billionaire inventor of a dark, sparkling drink, had he filed for a patent. He names it Kola-Cannelle (an additional ingredient being cinnamon), which he could abbreviate as 'Ko-Ca'. From Nha Trang he writes back to Roux: 'I have sent you by parcel post a bottle of Kola-Cannelle. Take approximately one and a half cubic centimetres of it in a glass of sugar water whenever you feel tired. I trust this "long-life elixir" will have the same re-invigorating effect on you as it does on me.'

Yersinia coca.

Tobacco, another plant headed for prohibition, is grown, as is the less threatened cassava. However, there are also failures, as Yersin lists in one of his notebooks: vanilla, nutmeg, gutta-percha and maize continue to resist acclimatisation. The estate harbours an agricultural and scientific community and includes a dispensary for the villagers. In the evenings, after closing his notebooks and scientific journals, Yersin dreams of the future of his realm of peace and prosperity and frets about rain. He knows how greedily the fields always absorb a good downpour.

One thinks of the hero of the Blaise Cendrars novel *Sutter's Gold*, Cendrars' Swiss fellow-countryman General John Sutter, ensconced in his Californian realm. At night, if time hangs heavy, Yersin might draw up plans for a water tower. And next morning he will set about erecting a water tower. Over the space of forty years he selects, in every corner of the world, all that is loveliest in nature and brings it back to Nha Trang – plants and animals, trees and flowers. The estate is not, at the time, earning anything from agriculture. The endless planting is a bottomless pit. Like Pasteur treating rabies, Yersin makes no attempt to patent his plague vaccine. Much as for those monks who, to fund their material needs, invent some liqueur or other, chartreuse or gentian, here a serum against rinderpest keeps heads above water. Soon a thousand doses a month are being sold to stockbreeders.

From time to time Yersin sends a paper to the *Annals of the Pasteur Institute*, the title of which is invariably laconic. 'Studies in certain epizootic diseases occurring in Indochina'. As a Parnassian poet, living in permanent retreat, might still offer the odd piece to the literary reviews. In France, modernist poetry has stopped using alexandrines. Yersin is ignorant of Apollinaire or Cendrars or of the latter's poems to the great Eiffel Tower of outer space. Nor is he aware that in Montparnasse, not far from the Paris Institute, Rivera and Soutine and Modigliani and Picasso will soon be rubbing shoulders. Painting and literature and all that crap – none of it touches Yersin's awareness, none of it. He is ensconced at Nha Trang, one eye glued to the microscope, or else, stick in hand, pacing his pastureland with giant strides.

Just like the rest of us, Yersin tries to make a fine, harmonious composition of his life.

The difference being that he succeeds.

Hanoi

Then a stroke of bad luck. A letter from Paul Doumer, the orphan from Aurillac, still governor general. Eight years since he discovered the plague bacillus, four years since he started his quiet life in Nha Trang. The new century is two years old. A babe. A little angel, no other word for it.

But this is about Doumer, and Doumer is going. They once climbed together up to Lang Bian Plateau, where Doumer promptly decided the Dalat Sanatorium should be built. They sailed up the Mekong together, from the delta to Phnom Penh. Now Doumer is leaving Asia. He is returning to France to resume his political career, stepping back into the lions' den. Where is the Russian crackpot Gorguloff at the time? Where is the hand of fate that, thirty years on, almost to the day, will bring the two face to face, the Russian émigré clutching the Browning that he is about to discharge into the Frenchman's chest?

Before coming to Hanoi to take up the post of governor general of the region that geographers, even Jules Ferry, are still calling 'Trans-Gangetic India', then 'Indo-China', and finally 'Indochina', back in Paris Doumer was a very young Minister of Finance from the radical left. He devised and ushered through parliament the first tax on income, to make the rich cough up. Out in this eastern posting, keen to leave his mark on colonial history, before going home he lays the first stone of a vast health complex of which he wants Yersin to take charge. A medical school and a laboratory attached to the Pasteur Institute, a hospital and a health centre. Doumer has spoken, so Yersin leaves Nha Trang for Hanoi.

He has not been back in the green and misty city for ages, not since his return from Sedang country with Father Guerlach and his subsequent interview with Lefèvre before leaving for Hong Kong. The new city of Hanoi is twenty years younger than that of Saigon. The French Tonkin authorities wasted no time. In a score of years that seem more like centuries, evincing the confidence and aplomb and sheer blindness of Romans adrift among Gauls, they build (for their own reassurance) the Hôtel Métropole and the Palais Puginier, inaugurate the racecourse and the covered food market, and clear and drain both lakes. The city already numbers seventy thousand inhabitants. Yersin has his Serpollet 5-CV embarked at Fishermen's Point; from Haiphong, a junk bears it up the Red River. This is the first automobile the capital has seen. Seated at the wheel, Yersin crawls up broad avenues under the shade of plane trees.

The finer districts are the first in Asia to be equipped with electricity, running water and street lighting. Scattered at random along quiet streets, columned and pedimented villas, painted white or ochre, sit behind well-kept gardens criss-crossed by raked paths. Half-timbered villas, their pointed gables rising beyond metal gates, protrude above darkly abundant vegetation. A Proustian city with nostalgic echoes of Cabourg or Deauville – even, in places, today.

Bicycle rickshaws give way to the hissing, spluttering machine. Carters adjust their horses' blinkers. Traders in conical hats, shoulders supporting a yoke, warily eye a vehicle that is too wide for the guild quarter's network of alleys. Where the old city meets the French city, not far from the Little Lake where the restored red Sword Pagoda rises, Yersin parks outside the entrance to the Métropole – still, more than a century on, the most comfortable hotel in what is now Vietnam's capital. The ghost of the future, the man with the moleskin-covered notebook, the one who has been on

Yersin's heels since Morges, who put up at the Zur Sonne in Marburg, the Royal in Phnom Penh, was with him when he met Calmette in a lounge at the Saigon Majestic, Emperor Bao Dai at the Lang Bian Palace in Dalat and Roux in the brasserie at the Lutetia, is sitting at the bar when Yersin signs his registration card at reception.

Doumer is already there with a drink and some plans unrolled in front of him.

Yersin presents no hint of masochism. Not for him, trekking for its own sake. He bears discomfort readily when he has to, the discomfort of the explorer's bivouac and of cold nights in the mountains. No stranger, he, to insect-ridden straw mats or even bare floors. But his preference, where comfort can be had, lies with the grade-A luxury of liner or palatial hotel.

From the Métropole he writes to Simond, who has now left India for Brazil. He wants to persuade the flea man to come and assist him in Hanoi, indeed take his place. The architect for the new medical school, he writes, 'estimates that the work will cost fifteen hundred thousand francs! Even so, that's a lot less expensive and far more useful than the Saigon Theatre.' He gives Simond time to think it over while conducting his yellow-fever research in the Americas. 'I was most interested in the details you gave me in your letter regarding your set-up in Petrópolis and the start of your work.'

As soon as the Hanoi buildings are ready, Yersin assumes command of the health complex, recruiting staff and organising admissions procedures for medical and nursing courses. He designs programmes on the French model, with bedside consultations at the hospital in the mornings and theory in the afternoons. He chooses to deliver the physics, chemistry and anatomy courses himself. One imagines the surprise Roux must have felt, remembering the dressing-down it had taken to make young Yersin agree to continue his microbiology course. But this is for Doumer, and Yersin gave his word.

At the end of the first year a cohort of eleven students are ready to take exams. 'Our medics have worked very hard. We have some who are quite excellent, in fact, as good as their finest French counterparts. Interestingly, even the brightest do a huge amount of work. One can almost say there are no shirkers at all.'

Yersin makes the occasional trip back to Nha Trang, where he continues to enlarge his domain while keeping a close eye on the growth of his rubber trees and monitoring vaccine production. In summer he leaves his room at the Métropole and books passage for Marseilles. He takes with him a fisherman's son, Que, whom he has turned into a mechanic. They have an appointment with Léon Serpollet himself, the world's first industrial producer of automobiles. On the road between Paris and Beauvais the three of them, hair blowing in the wind, clock one hundred kilometres an hour in the new Serpollet 6-CV, an absolutely modern breed of racer that persuades Yersin, already a fan, to place an order for one, arranging to have it delivered straight to Hanoi.

After two years of management and administration, with everything running smoothly, Yersin feels he can at last resign.

He has done two years' research at the Institut Pasteur in Paris, served for two years as a ship's doctor for the Messageries Maritimes line, and now he will have directed the Hanoi hospital for two years. He tires of things swiftly – all bar Nha Trang. Doumer has gone. Later, the big bridge over the Red River will bear his name, the Paul Doumer Bridge, today's Long Bien.

Yersin, now over forty, is past yomping. In the calm of maturity, he turns to honing other skills. His life in Hanoi will have been a mere episode – which others would deem the start of a hospital career, a future as the big cheese in the white coat. It takes several more months to sort out his succession. After nearly three years in Hanoi, he returns to Nha Trang, following a further stay in Paris and a final trip to Morges. One last time, he gives old Fanny a hug in the little chintz parlour of Fig Tree House on the shore of the Lake. She dies the following year.

It has turned five, the new century. The scoundrel century. So far, so good. It is blooming. Difficult to picture the torturers and executioners as beaming infants. The monster-to-be is now five years old. Fanny dies in the same year as Jules Verne, the same year as Brazza, too, whose body is brought back from Dakar to Marseilles. But the century is already evincing grave tendencies, as Yersin himself records: 'There is reason to wonder whether war between Britain and Germany is not imminent. Let's hope France will not be involved!' Russia's first revolution occurs, and Trotsky, in St Petersburg, assumes command of the soviets. The Nobel Prize goes to the great lama Koch. Ten years have passed since Pasteur's death. In Paris, Yersin is reunited with Paul Doumer, whose career is advancing towards the man's tragic destiny. He is now Chairman of the National Assembly.

Yersin writes to his sister Émilie, mainly to inform her that he renounces his share of the inheritance, the young bags' money. Some sisters are as solicitous as mothers, and the correspondence survives. However, it comprises fewer letters, and they are shorter, less intimate and less detailed – except as regards chickens.

The unmarried sister, the female Yersin, having first studied piano and absorbed the fine manners of Fig Tree House, thinks that, rather than marry well, she will use her bit of capital to build a chalet in Bellevue, up above the Lake, where she sees herself breeding marmots or keeping bees – her choice eventually settles on aviculture. She is forty-five. Yersin, the confirmed bachelor, after his several-year medical interlude in Hanoi, resumes his old fads at Nha Trang. Apples never fall far from the tree, they say, and the fads to which both brother and sister adhere are those of their father, the teacher in the black frockcoat and top hat, torn between the gunpowder industry and the nervous system of the field cricket.

the chicken controversy

The history of science is often rolled out as a broad avenue leading straight from ignorance to truth, but that is false. The history of science is a network of dead ends in which thought loses its way and ties itself up in knots. An anthology of pitiful failures, some quite ridiculous. Not unlike the early days of aviation in that respect. Which themselves coincided with the early days of cinema. Those jerky black-and-white films showing wood smashing and canvas tearing. Men in tutus with dreams of being Icarus and wings harnessed to their upper bodies, running towards the edge of a cliff with arms outstretched in the manner of ballerinas, leaping into the void and falling like stones to smash on the beach below.

Émilie squanders the young bags' money on hens. She invests her modest crust in having a large model chicken house built and fitted out at nearby Lonay. Yersin tries to dissuade her. It's like pissing in the wind. They are like twins, those two: their obstinacy knows no bounds. Émilie becomes the first person in Europe to import from America an absolutely modern granular chicken food called 'Full-o'-Pep'. She performs experiments, recording the results in a notebook each day: numbers of eggs and weights of hens sold for the table. She contributes columns to country magazines, *La Vie à la campagne* and *La Terre vaudoise*.

Although particularly partial to hen's eggs, which together with vegetables form the core of his diet, Yersin previously paid scant attention to his own poultry, those small, grey, anonymous-looking Annamite birds scratching at liberty in the earth in front of his house – but banned absolutely from the vegetable garden. Now he sees them through different eyes, and the gaze they return is somehow different, too. They blink as they look at him now, between that nodding of lowered heads that resembles a mechanical pulse, newly aware that he wants something of them, that they are about to become scientific subjects. Pasteurians, as we know, owe a great deal to hens. Yersin determines to improve the local strain by cross-breeding. His sister sends him a large Vaudois cockerel for his little Annamite hens. Here, no doubt, we should consult the Freudian crowd about this decidedly incestuous piece of procurement. The little hens are rather flustered, having failed to see this coming. They acquire quite a taste for scientific research.

Yet enough is not, in this instance, enough. The microscope has to come out once more, as do the scientific journals. Seated at his desk, still in his cane chair, Yersin studies embryology, notably Haeckel's law whereby the development of a single being (ontogeny) recapitulates in the embryology of the chick that of the entire species (phylogeny). Inside the egg, in speeded-up form, the foetus lopes through the evolution of the Galliformes from the reptile onwards. Loving eggs as he does, loving his sister as he does, Yersin wants to know how, with yolk and white of egg, one arrives at a beak, feathers, feet, and before long, on the plate, the wing, the thigh, sometimes with chips. Having once addressed a problem, he does nothing by halves. Up go the sleeves of his white coat, rolled to the elbow. He must always know it all, Yersin, he can do no other. The man who vanquished plague is not going to let a chicken defeat him.

The correspondence grows, each continuing his or her experiments at opposite ends of the earth. Émilie goes mad about the xograph, a recent entry in France's *Concours*

Lépine, a competition for inventions. The inventor in this instance, the Nostradamus of aviculture, claims that his appliance means that eggs can be sexed from the moment of laying. Yersin is dubious. 'This gadget strikes me as being in the same category as seance tables and suchlike trick devices. One would need to know on what principle it rests.' He orders two himself, and he and his zoology assistant, Armand Krempf, undertake a scientific study using the statistical method.

He starts to take a huge interest in incubation. Doing nothing by halves, as usual, he designs an aviary two hundred metres square and ten metres high. He imports Blue Leghorn pullets and Indian cockerels, buys a Spratt electric incubator, devises laying boxes and perches.

The two men keep daily records of numbers of eggs laid and their weight, take measurements with a micrometer, describe the deformities of certain hatchlings. And this giant of science, whom Roux and Pasteur had been unable to keep at their side, the genius of microbiology who, once he deigns to set his hand to the task, solves the riddles of that discipline in two shakes of a lamb's tail, is now to be found within the four walls of his henhouse, up to the ankles of his rubber boots in straw and chicken shit. Taking turns, each with furrowed brow, Yersin and Krempf swing the little pendulum above the numbered egg, write down in a notebook what the Nostradamus of aviculture predicts, and carefully deposit the egg in the Spratt incubator as in a Christmas crib.

And every twenty-one days there is joyous havoc as tiny beaks tap eggshells open. The two Pasteurian magi catch chicks before they can scarper and their numbers be forgotten. And what are they looking for, those wise men in white coats with a magnifying-glass in one hand and a ball of fluff in the other? A tiny prick, two tiny tits, heaven knows. Anyway, it fails to work. The xograph is a con, told you so, it would miss the one hatchling that goes on to lay golden eggs. Want my advice? Shove the thing in a cupboard or donate it to the village kids, they'll find a use for it.

While they wade in droppings in Nha Trang, back in Paris Nobel Prizes begin to rain down on the Pasteurians. Laveran is recognised for his work on malaria. Metchnikoff for his research into the immune system. Yersin winds up his avian experiments and records his conclusions, sending a copy to Émilie. To obtain the best layers in Indochina, he recommends crossing Annamites with Wyandottes. He invents a balanced poultry food that is far better than America's Full-o'-Pep (cheaper, too) and adapted for use in Switzerland, a blend based on bean flour, dried blood and powdered mimosa leaf. He writes a paper on it, but that's not going to win him a Nobel.

an ark

Yersin's magnificent folly is biblical, possibly. It is rooted in distant memories of canonical readings in the Morges Free Evangelical Church. There comes a time when nomadic man ceases his journeying and settles down, the hunter-gatherer becomes stockbreeder or arable farmer. Abel or Cain. Reaching the age when his father squashed that last cricket with his falling brow, Yersin probably thought it was his turn now. Or perhaps, generalising from Haeckel's law, he posited that everyone, over the course of his or her existence, reca-pitulates the history of humanity in accelerated form. A susceptibility to aneurysm is not hereditary. He has now lived longer than his father. He and his ark have dropped anchor here in Nha Trang for however many years remain to him. Precisely how many he does not know.

Seated at his desk in his cane chair, Yersin consults engineering reviews and veterinary journals. He writes off to Paris or Switzerland: one day he is importing Norman or Dutch rabbits, another day it is a meridian circle, or a Serpollet steamboat, or a phonograph with dozens of music rolls, or it might be a Ditisheim recording chronometer. And each time the boat calls in at the bay the Ali Baba hold is unloaded, a crew of sailors row towards Fishermen's Point out of a purple sunset, and a line of porters, bearing bundles and crates on their heads, advance along the jetty towards Dr Nam's house, where the doctor awaits them in the shelter of the veranda. An inventory of his gear, with one notable exception, will be found at the end of a letter signed *Rimbaud* and written from *Aden, Arabia*: 'I want the finest of everything manufactured in France (or elsewhere overseas) in the way of instruments for mathematics, optics, astronomy, electricity, meteorology, pneumatics, mechanics, hydraulics and mineralogy. I am not bothered about surgical instruments.'

Seated at a table in the shelter of his veranda, facing the splendour of the sun-filled bay, Yersin slowly finishes his eggs and vegetables (he eats little meat and drinks only water) and puts down his napkin. The dishes he consumes will surely have that wonderful tang of *rau ram* leaves. The rest of the day he devotes to animal husbandry and agriculture. A worthy bearer of the fine title *paysan*, Yersin resides in the *paysage*, the countryside, far from Baudelaire's 'mocking world' and 'vile masses'. With the meticulous attention to detail of his entomologist father and the towering ambition of the empire builder, Yersin labours away at extending his domain, following the example of the Portuguese plantation owners still to be found in São Tomé and Príncipe. There is already a long ribbon of cultivated land sloping down from the foothills of the Annamite sierra to Nha Trang, a representative sample of climates, a vertical hacienda, a grand carpet that he hopes one day to see unfurl from the mountains to the sea. It reaches higher each day, grows ever wider as more and more stations open. As each plot is wrested from the jungle, it is immediately sown for grazing.

Agricultural teams multiply. A village is laid out at Suoi Giao, now midway between the Institute and its latest plantations. No one had thought to live there before. Virgin land sprouts houses on stilts, barns for drying tobacco, a chemistry lab with accommodation for research staff. Yersin has his own bungalow built there, designs a model communal system, a classical republic, suggests to hunter-gatherers that they become farmers, raise stock. Cain, or Abel. He clears a hundred hectares for them to grow mountain rice. He plants linseed, too – for weaving cloth.

And for dressing savages with ingenuous probity.

an outpost of progress

People start to accuse him of doing too much at once. Their complaints are not entirely unjustified. The man who discovered the plague bacillus and invented the anti-plague vaccine should be in Paris or Geneva, heading a laboratory or running a hospital. Yersin should be a leading medical expert at the Academy of Sciences, a top boffin. Instead, they say, he has withdrawn to a fishing village on the other side of the world. He refuses to see journalists, so they have no choice but to make things up, embellish the dark legend.

He is rumoured to spend some of his time alone in a shack, tripping over his hermit's beard. He is described as the mad king of an idiot people on whom he conducts cruel experiments to make the mind boggle. A nabob, using science to perform conjuring tricks for simple-minded warriors, proclaiming himself their heaven-sent chief. A tyrant exploiting the 'magic' of gas and electricity as a pretext for enslaving a few bloodthirsty tribesmen, who bow down before him and sacrifice virgins in his honour. A Kurtz or a Mayréna, a loner as far out of his mind as he is far from home. Granted, the first ice cube smashed with a hammer in Nha Trang must have bewildered many. Emerging from the gas-fired Pictet machine, the white bed of strange, sparkling shards that burnt the hand but kept fish fresh till next day – they will have been quite as dazzling as when a couple of them fed the five thousand on the shore at Galilee.

Yersin allies the miracles of modernity to his own fondness for things mechanical, for grease and adjustable spanners as much as for the syringe and the microscope. He is as happy in blue overalls as in a white coat. And as the first car driver locally, clearly he has to open the first service station. 'I've just completed the new adjustments to my Serpollet 6-CV. I tried it out yesterday and it ran to perfection. Today I began fitting out the boat, which will take me most of a fortnight, then there'll be the standing engine to assemble that is going to operate a water pump for the lab, then my old Serpollet 5-CV to repair, and finally two more repairs: my motorcycle and the water-mill. Suddenly I'm an engineer!'

In contrast to the story of the mad scientist wandering the jungle, what keeps Yersin busy in those years leading up to the First World War is entirely peaceful and, to the uninitiated, actually rather daunting. He places his gift for observation, his extreme precision, his taste for figures and his manic punctuality at the service of the construction camp for the railway line that will link Nha Trang and Phan Rang. Those places have a reputation as slaughterhouses: one death per sleeper, the story goes.

Conrad, on reaching the Congo, where he would write *An Outpost of Progress* and *Heart of Darkness*, had described the horror of the works site when the Belgians were building a railway from Stanley Pool to the Atlantic. Daguerches, in his novel *Kilomètre 83*, had described the slaughter that went on in the French works site of the Siam–Cambodia railway. Yersin meets Noël Bernard, the doctor in charge of the health department who later heads the Saigon Pasteur Institute and goes on to be his first biographer as well as Calmette's. Yersin is able to reconcile his own agoraphobia with a need for fraternity. Together with his new assistant and follower, Dr Vassal, fresh from vaccinating plague victims on Réunion, he receives patients from the camp in Nha Trang. The two men take samples, study typhus and malaria. 'We are once more seeing a full-scale cholera epidemic. My mechanic is currently dying of this filthy disease, against which we are so helpless.'

*

And then, once yearly, while the harvest ripens and his team of young technicians (chemists, zoologists, bacteriologists, agronomists) pursue their work, Yersin boards the *Paul Lecat*, the latest flagship of the Messageries Maritimes line, and sails away to the luxury of the Lutetia. He takes a trip to the French capital, in other words. The mystery man of science, the explorer emerging from his jungle hideout, strolls unrecognised through the streets of Paris.

Only his Pasteurian friends know him, as does his friend Serpollet. This brilliant handyman, holder of the first driving licence in France, probably in the world, the first industrial manufacturer of automobiles, even if they are all built to commission, is bringing out a Serpollet 11-CV that will mark the pinnacle of his career. Afterwards Armand Peugeot buys up Serpollet Motors and opens his own factory, followed by the young Louis Renault, and the Serpollet brand disappears with Léon Serpollet. A marvellous statue by Jean Boucher stands in place St Ferdinand in Paris's seventeenth arrondissement. They are quite a pair, Yersin and Serpollet, doing 100 kilometres an hour down the Beauvais road. After his friend's death, Yersin buys a Clément-Bayard 15-CV, passing from steam cars to petrol cars, then a Torpédo Zèbre, and then one day nothing, he has done cars, he has a new idea, he wants an aeroplane.

No one knows it at the time, but those years are already ripe for numbering backwards, to measure out the time left to run before the '14 disaster. In 1910 – or Minus Four – the Lutetia opens at last. Yersin chooses the corner room on the sixth floor, a clear view of the Eiffel Tower. He has an appointment at Chartres aerodrome that summer. He wants to try out an aeroplane, which means donning flying suit, mitts and large goggles. He finds his first attempt rather unsettling all the same, lands with trembly legs and writes to Émilie: 'Those things are still at the stage of being dangerous toys.' He admires the courage of Louis Blériot, who the year before flew solo across the English Channel in one of these kite-machines. He discusses prices but defers the plan for lack of landing strips in Indochina. He could build his own in Nha Trang, of course, but having only one strip would limit him to local flying – a boring prospect.

Two years later, in Minus Two, plague reappears in China. Yersin fears it may be like Bombay all over again. 'There are too many doctors in situ already. Still, I've written to Roux to say that, should he see the slightest advantage for the Pasteur Institute in my going to Manchuria, he has only to telegraph me and I shall leave immediately.' In the following year, Minus One, Albert Schweitzer departs to open his African hospital in Lambarene, which will earn him a Nobel. He finances his work with the proceeds of his organ recitals and later with his Bach records. In Yersin's case, at that point in time, the funds come from rubber.

He has turned planter. Substantial money is beginning to accrue. Enough to keep his Institute going. Then really big returns. Quite a gold mine, in fact. From successfully anticipating the rise of the car and the bicycle. He deposits the cash in a safe at the Hong Kong Shanghai Bank, buys shares. Then along comes '14. Gaston Calmette is assassinated in his *Figaro* office. Jean Jaurès is assassinated in his café. July arrives, bringing Sarajevo. Four years of trench warfare and mustard gas follow. Yersin sends the occasional consignment of rubber to Clermont-Ferrand. He himself stays put in his paradise, extending its boundaries, further increasing its beauty.

the king of rubber

He is Annam's first cyclist, Annam's first motorcyclist, Annam's first motorist, so it stands to reason that he should also become Annam's first rubber producer. Since his time in Madagascar he has been combing the scientific journals, monitoring advances in industry and mechanics, developing a fascination for everything modern, absolutely modern, and the inflatable rubber tyre is a case in point.

Ever since La Condamine and his little group of Enlightenment scientists were sent to Ecuador in the eighteenth century, it has been known that South-American Indians harvest latex. They use the resultant gum to waterproof and caulk vessels. They seek out wild heveas growing at random in the green inferno of Amazonia. The British, having pilfered seeds in Brazil, sow them in orderly rows in Ceylon. Dutchmen do likewise in Java. Here too the conflict soon becomes political and geostrategic. Yersin goes to look at Java.

From Batavia he proceeds to Buitenzorg. 'The agriculture is admirable, the people gentle. Moreover, with its many volcanoes the island has so many natural curiosities that they alone would make it an interesting place to visit.' He visits Malaysian plantations in Malacca, selects *Hevea brasiliensis* seeds. At the time when Yersin plants his first rubber trees, Goodyear's invention of vulcanisation is fifty years old, Dunlop's inflatable rubber tyre ten years old. Yersin plants some hundred hectares initially. By the time war breaks out, two tons of latex are being produced each month. A contract is signed with the ingenious Michelin. Before long the number of hectares has increased to three hundred. A gold mine indeed. Yersin is efficient, his approach rational.

His success also owes much to his encounter with Vernet, an agronomist sent out to Asia by French seed giant Vilmorin to collect plants. Yersin, whose gifts include surrounding himself with people who know more than him and listening to what they say, takes him on. Not content with being the first rubber planter in Annam, Yersin is keen to conduct an agronomical study. The two men design protocols, write articles on the chemical composition of soils, fertiliser trials, seed collection and techniques of coagulating latex and tapping in the laticiferous tubes. Experiments are carried out that involve sacrificing some trees by stripping off all or part of their foliage. The conclusion is that 'the proportion of gum contained in latex depends to a great extent on chlorophyl function: in other words, leaves may be said to perform the principal role in elaborating rubber.'

The two men invent an appliance called a 'picnodilamometer' (it works better than the xograph, this one) designed to measure the density of latex and its gum content. They draw up calculation tables. Then they fall out. Yersin complains to Calmette: 'Vernet is a dreadful character, immensely vain, as stubborn as a mule, and with a wholly illogical mind.' Deciding to deal directly with the Clermont-Ferrand expert in future, Yersin asks him to second one of his engineers to work under him in Nha Trang. 'Michelin is definitely the smartest man when it comes to rubber.' He also wants the backing of the Pasteurians. 'So I have written a letter to Michelin, using Mr Roux as an intermediary.'

But Europe is at war, and Roux has other things to think about. He is being sent to the front on a health mission. The Pasteur Institute and the Koch Institute on the other side of the line, drawn into the conflict, have placed themselves at the disposal of their respective high commands. Yersin finds himself isolated. France does not reply. Taking up his pilgrim's staff, he resumes his expeditions in the mountains in the company of Armand Krempf. Starting from Suoi Giao, after two days on the water and two days spent climbing, they pitch their tent at high altitude, and discover Hon Ba Hill, where it is cool and rainy.

In a matter of months a weather station has been set up there, acclimatisation trials conducted involving several plant and animal species, and ground prepared and sown. The temperature there goes down to six degrees Celsius, and in winter the hill is covered in dense fog. No more mosquitoes. A foaming stream. Yersin has himself a Swiss chalet built in the chilly jungle. 'I have telegraphed Mr Roux to ask him whether I might usefully serve in France during the war. I await his reply.' The reply is that he should stay in Asia.

He knows he can no longer travel, that he must give up the Lutetia and the *Paul Lecat*. The war or his quarrel with Vernet has worsened his misanthropy. He starts spending several weeks on end up at Hon Ba, living like a hermit in his hilltop chalet, drawing water from the stream, thinking, seeing no one, entirely silent, splitting his own logs. Like the 'Young Rousselle' of French folk song, Yersin now has three houses in three different climatic environments, all without leaving his own estate, which already covers five thousand hectares and will eventually triple in size. The war has dragged on for almost two years now. The Battle of Verdun is being fought. Yersin sits in his chalet. Studying ornithology and horticulture. Filling notebooks. 'I have a number of Japanese chrysanthemums in flower at the moment. They have huge blooms, dishevelled, superb. I take real pleasure in marvelling at them.'

With time hanging heavy on his hands, perhaps, he conceives a fresh fascination for orchids, collecting them, managing to obtain new specimens in lands that the war leaves untouched, countries whose flags are respected by belligerent fleets. From Central America, across the Pacific, he imports rare Costa Rican varieties to Nha Trang, he builds a vast glasshouse, setting up his photographic apparatus at the centre of it. A Richard Verascope. In his darkroom he produces his first colour pictures. From his decades of taking photographs, hundreds upon hundreds of shots that virtually no one has ever seen still await viewing in the dimly lit archives of the Pasteur Institute in Paris.

In front of his house he has planted a fig tree, a cutting that Émilie sent from Fig Tree House in Morges. He studies arboriculture, learns pruning and layering, prepares grafts for his fruit trees, acclimatises apple and plum. 'The apricot dislikes the wet season even more than the peach.' He tries to dissuade villagers from pursuing their slash-and-burn policy, an ecological disaster that nevertheless imparts that lovely smoky taste to the forest rice that grows in the ashes. He launches a reforestation campaign. With the help of his little Nha Trang crowd he lists and describes the endemic tree species – *lims, cam xe, giong huong*. The local teak is good only for cutting fence posts for animal corrals. Nurseries are dug, kilometre-long trenches filled with rotting leaves and topsoil.

He goes on writing all this down in letters he sends to the Pasteur Institute in Paris, as if continuing with the Pasteurians the kind of diary he once kept for Fanny's benefit. He writes to Roux: 'Growing flowers delights me more and more. I should like to cover the whole mountaintop with them, and one day I hope to do so. I am trying Alpines, I've already got bilberries coming up, and I have sown some small blue gentians, which I am keeping an anxious eye on.' One can just see Roux shrugging at that 'anxious'. Or hear the strained laughter prompted by memories of apocalyptic shellfire and shattered corpses rotting on barbed wire. Roux on a few days' leave from the front, his uniform splattered with mud and blood, the red cross on his armband, opening the stack of letters from Yersin, his colleague fretting over his small blue gentians.

First the sea and the mountains, now flowers.

Why not little birds?

Yersin is indeed building aviaries, gathering budgerigars and parrots about him. He has exotic birds sent from all quarters, releases them in his orchid houses.

The Pasteurians stop listening to him, and he begins a correspondence with Henry Correvon of the botanical gardens in Yverdon, Switzerland. From Correvon he orders seeds and seeks advice. His earliest biographers mention the cattleyas and hibiscus at Nha Trang, the amaryllis and parrot's beak impatiens. Higher up, at Suoi Giao, amaranths and violets, verbena and arum, cyclamen and fuchsia. At Hon Ba, roses and orchids. In his letters Yersin lists plants that come into leaf but never flower: stocks, hyacinths, narcissi, tulips. He studies botany. Flowers are the sex organs of plants, he reads.

Maybe, like him, these have decided never to reproduce.

He is aware of the twaddle that newspapers invent. He has read the silly stories about his dark secrets, how he is accused of fathering a child, how some mountain native has borne a son to Dr Nam. A woman from one of those tribes among which neither the Republic nor the Emperor of Annam has ever bothered to conduct a census. There will be other such stories. It never rains but it pours. More probably, Yersin is already beyond the pathetic gestures of reproduction. He has spent quite enough time in labs coupling males in rut with females in heat, rubbing the muzzles of rats against the vulvae of ratesses to speed up the experiment, and among the bugs in his dishes he has never identified a bacillus called love. No doubt he entertains a healthy scorn for the lures and fornications that multiply lives for no good reason.

Yersin will travel no more. He has been all over the globe and seen both sides of every question. He knows the globe is shrinking, things are becoming the same everywhere, soon one must fear Rimbaud's 'same bourgeois magic wherever the mailboat drops us off'. He is a tree now. Being a tree is a life, too, and it does not involve moving on. He is approaching that fine, infinite solitude. That marvellous listlessness. And in the evenings, when tiredness makes enthusiasms pale, when a man kicks his heels without even the consolation of drink, he'll have a good talk about it with Dad – ask his father's advice. Remember: one is now much older than the old man ever was. This is the final stretch before death. One knows a thing or two about decomposition. Here is the soil he wants to decompose in.

Many an evening, up at the chalet, alone with his Siamese cats, he rereads Pasteur. 'If microscopic creatures disappeared from the globe, the surface of the earth would be littered with dead organic matter and corpses of all kinds, animal and vegetable. It is chiefly they that give oxygen its oxidant properties. Without them life would become impossible, for the work of death would be incomplete.' It is life, Yersin reflects, seeking to live, that yearns to quit this ageing body as quickly as possible in order to leap into a fresh body – and it is life, transitory life, that rewards such bodies with the pence of orgasm for their involuntary contribution to its continuance. Nothing is born of nothing. All that is born must die. We are all, between birth and death, at liberty to lead the calm, upright life of the mounted horseman. The ancient Stoicism that Spinoza reflects, and the immanent force of life, which alone lives on. That pure principle, that ever-nascent nature around which everything, having turned, returns. Life is the farce we must all perform.

He broods briefly, and the war goes on and on. For almost four years now two brother peoples have waged mutual destruction, hurling thousands upon thousands of their children into the dustbin of the trenches. He will doubtless never see peace again, never revisit Paris or Berlin. Victory hangs in the balance. Clemenceau and Roux, both of them doctors, pace the front line.

to posterity

When Yersin lays down his bedside book, the towering figure of the Commander of the Legion of Honour looms in the darkness. In frockcoat and bow tie, blue of eye and furrowed of brow. The shadowed mouth repeats words that Yersin knows by rote: 'Plague being a disease of which we are wholly ignorant of the cause, it is not illogical to suppose that this disease too may be produced by a particular microbe. All experimental research being necessarily guided by certain preconceived ideas, one might easily (and perhaps very usefully) approach the study of this disease in the belief that it is parasitic.' When Pasteur penned those words, setting out bacterial theory as a working hypothesis, Yersin was seventeen years old. Still an overly serious pupil, musing under the lime trees of Morges secondary school. Five years before the first anti-rabies vaccination. Fourteen before the discovery of the bacillus in Hong Kong.

Pasteur might have invented him from scratch, manipulating Yersin's life like that of a laboratory animal. As if the elderly hemiplegic, unable to travel himself, sent him out to Hong Kong in his place, sent Yersin's younger arms and legs, Yersin's young blue eyes and above all Yersin's youthful mind, which he himself had trained to observe. As if Yersin's purpose were to realise a prophecy of Pasteur's, right down to the accident that, by depriving him of an incubator in Hong Kong, had led him to discover the bacillus at ambient temperature, beating Kitasato to it, the rival who mistakenly conducted his own study at the temperature of the human body. As if the discovery itself simply illustrated something that Pasteur had written long before: 'In the field of observation, chance favours only the mind made ready.'

Yersin is a double, a clone of the junior crystallographer who criss-crosses Europe during his country's Second Empire, writing with passion: 'I shall go to Trieste, I shall go to the ends of the Earth. I have to discover the source of racemic acid.' The young Pasteur leaps into cabs and onto trains, from Vienna to Leipzig, to Dresden and Munich and

Prague, conducts his experiments in garrets and attics, hefts a suitcase laden with test tubes and pipettes and syringes and the microscope that is the eye of our eye, climbs the Sea of Ice above Chamonix to collect samples of pure air.

And Yersin comes to realise that the man who, though never a medic himself, will turn the whole history of medicine on its head, would in fact have made a good explorer, he had a feeling for it, and that feeling came across in the images he used to describe his research. 'In progressively discovering the unknown the scientist is akin to a traveller as he scales higher and higher peaks and scans ever greater expanses still to be explored.'

A decade or so before his death Pasteur visited Edinburgh in the company of Ferdinand de Lesseps, and the two men, both at the height of their fame, paid a visit to the daughter of Livingstone, the doctor and explorer – and a 'pastor' himself. Several years later Pasteur invited Yersin to dine with him after the latter's lecture at the French Geographical Society and quizzed him on his explorations, had read Yersin's report on his journey to the country of the Moi people and immediately penned those enthusiastic letters of recommendation, placing his enormous prestige at the service of someone who had actually had a bellyful of scientific research and was in the process of quitting the Pasteurian crowd altogether. To thank the old man, Yersin sent him a fine carved elephant's tusk, which still hangs on the wall of Pasteur's apartment, now a museum.

Lying alone at night in his Hon Ba chalet, far from the bombing, over fifty years old, Yersin harbours no illusions as to his own fame, not any more. He knows full well that all he will leave behind are two Latin words, *Yersinia pestis*, with which only doctors will be familiar.

Nor did the two theses written by the young Pasteur – one in chemistry, 'Investigations into the saturation capacity of arsenic acid', the other in physics, an 'Examination of some phenomena relating to rotary polarisation of liquids' – demonstrate any great desire for instant popular success.

Pasteur's teacher was Jean-Baptiste Biot. As a student, Pasteur attended Biot's induction ceremony at the French Academy and heard his speech, the wise old mage exhorting young scientists to dedicate themselves to pure research:

The masses may be ignorant of your name, indeed of your very existence. But you will be recognised, respected and sought out by a small number of eminent men scattered throughout the globe, your emulators and peers in the world senate of intelligent minds that alone has the right to award you a rank, a deserved rank, from which neither ministerial influence nor princely will nor the whim of the people can ever topple you, any more than they were able to raise you to that height, a rank that will endure for as long as you remain loyal to the science that bestows it upon you.

And years later it is old Pasteur's turn to write his induction speech, to don the green coat, sheath his sword and pay tribute to Littré, the great positivist, biographer of Auguste Comte, the lexicologist who chose to give the French language the new words *microbe* and *microbie*. The beginning of Pasteur's text presents itself as an exercise in modesty: 'Yet again I am struck by a sense of my own inadequacy, and I should be embarrassed to find myself in this position were it not my duty to hand to science itself the honour – the impersonal honour, one might term it – that you have done me.' As usual the matter is more complex and the modesty wholly rhetorical.

It conceals enormous pride. Pasteur devotes years to erecting a statue to himself. With that inordinate French predilection for pomp and monumentalism, for glory and political squabbling. That indissoluble blend of universalism and sacred love of country that prompted Louis Pasteur, son of a dyed-in-the-wool Bonapartist turned fervent republican, to write as a young student: 'How those magic words liberty and fraternity and that revival of the Republic, burgeoning in the warm sun of our twentieth year, filled our heart with strange, unheralded and utterly delicious feelings!'

All these quirks of politics, totally strange to Yersin, move

Pasteur to seek, at the height of his fame, popular electoral backing in a bid for election to the Senate – in which bid he fails. Yersin knows all about Pasteur's infinitely time-wasting squabbles with doctors, with spontaneous generation, and with Pouchet, Liebig and Koch. The statue carved in the man's lifetime with the hammer and chisel of diatribes and newspaper articles. The interminable quarrels at the Academy of Sciences and the Academy of Medicine. The system of sealed envelopes to ensure the anteriority of his discoveries, the last left unopened until the late twentieth century. His *honoris causa* degree torn up and sent back to Bonn after Sedan and the bombs dropped on Paris, the 1871 Treaty of Frankfurt as monstrous as the Treaty of Versailles was to become later. The political backing of the British, of Lister, the surgeon, and the words uttered by physiologist Huxley at London's Royal Society to the effect that 'Pasteur's discoveries would suffice on their own to cover the war ransom of five billion paid by France to Germany.' Rather than which the Republic, he says, should pay a pension to the ruined benefactor of mankind. Yet Pasteur will leave a name on the historical record that Yersin will not.

Yersin well knows that he is a dwarf.

Quite a big dwarf, though.

To win a place in posterity he should have invented an item of general consumption. Because the twentieth century, besides being one of barbarism, is to be one of registered trademarks. Justus von Liebig, Charles Goodyear, John Boyd Dunlop, André and Édouard Michelin, Armand Peugeot, Louis Renault. People would forget only their forenames.

Had Yersin called his drink not Ko-Ca but Yersinia and marketed it properly, his name would shine still.

So there he lies, alone at night in his Hon Ba chalet. By his age, Pasteur and his father had both succumbed long since to their respective cerebral haemorrhages. Old Pasteur awaited his death in a chaise longue, living in retirement at Villeneuve-l'Étang, an Institute property that the Pasteurians still referred to as the Garche annexe at the heart of the commune of Marnes-la-Coquette (which retains all its charm today), surrounded by nature, beneath the tall park trees. The time: summer. Sun plays in the foliage. Circles of light flit to and fro over the grass. Pasteur is serene, anticipating a state funeral with a service in Notre-Dame. Everything has been arranged with Roux. They will even, for him, dispense with the promiscuity of the Panthéon. A Pharaonic crypt is to receive his body in the Institute basement. Gilded marble columns and Byzantine mosaics. He mulls over the old words that will punctuate his funeral oration. Joy, valour, uprightness.

Together, they echo the ethic of the old philosopher, simple and, all in all, not so bad: act in such a way that the rule governing your action can be seen as a universal rule governing all action.

fruit and veg

Next morning, Yersin wakes in silence and peacefulness. He is pleased to have managed to acclimatise potatoes up here at the chalet – potatoes, strawberries and raspberries. Green beans and lettuce. Beetroot and carrots. 'A couple of days ago I ate the first peach to ripen at Hon Ba.' The soil is rich and red beneath green grass. A century on, the Dalat region still lives off the horticulture and vegetables imported by Yersin. It sends artichokes and gladioli all over Vietnam. Not surprisingly, his portrait overlooks the Lake. Not surprisingly, his name is a thousand times better known here than in Paris.

*

Returning to Nha Trang, he sits down at his short-wave radio set and listens to the appalling casualty figures coming out of Chemin-des-Dames, hears about chemical weapons. As if life, back there, is in black and white and here explodes in a thousand colours. He has signed up to receive the Havas and Reuter telegrams. After the war, it appears, Russia and America may well partition a ruined Europe, ruling over fields laid waste, the soil of the whole European countryside churned up like that of Verdun, divvying up the mud, gas fumes, dead trees. As if back there the Apocalypse has arrived and his mission is to salvage the beauty of Europe aboard his Asian ark.

Sending letters is becoming a random business. He feels increasingly isolated. 'My dear sister, it has been ages since I heard from you. Several letters must be missing. They probably went down in the Mediterranean.' Yersin keeps records of the names of ships of the Marseille–Saigon line torpedoed by the Germans and the dates when they disappeared. The *Ville de la Ciotat*, the *Magellan*, then the *Athos*, sent to the bottom with its cargo of latex from Suoi Giao, the *Australien* …

All the young men have left for the front. A handful of elderly Pasteurians are stranded in Vietnam. Simond, the flea man, has quit Brazil for the Pasteur Institute in Saigon. Yersin persuades him to share his own love of orchids, his love of photography, and the two resume their correspondence. 'I have written to Lumière, ordering fresh plates. I shall hear from him within a month, I expect, and can let you know whether he will go on making autochrome plates or whether the war will bring production to a halt.'

He tells Simond that he is leaving on a hike with Krempf 'to photograph some interesting Nui Chua Chan orchids *in situ*'. In the same letter he once again complains of his 'dark secrets', the journalistic tittle-tattle about his sex life – which in fact, like Krempf's, appears to have been of a purely hygienist nature.

Then we shall visit the Celibatorium of which I am still worthy, because the story of my marriage to an Englishwoman is a vicious rumour!

I should very much like to know what has become of Calmette. I've had no news of him since war was declared, and I don't know where to reach him, Lille being still under German occupation.

Warmest regards ...

In one of his notebooks Yersin lists the plants that still resist his ingenuity, refuse to leave Europe behind and strike root in his corner of Asia: currant bushes, walnut trees, almond trees. And above all, of course, the grapevine. He copies the list in a letter to Correvon in Vaud, which he knows may never reach its Swiss destination. He closes the notebook labelled

Agriculture, opens the one on epizootic diseases, then the *Aviculture* one, then closes them all, frowning. A new idea had just occurred to him. This happens every five minutes. He starts a letter to the governor general: 'I am thinking we might organise a collection here assembling the chief varieties of exotic ornamental tree fern. It would help to develop our lovely mountain station into a proper national park.'

The envelope is sealed and placed on the stack of mail waiting for the next boat to call. But next moment he has an even better idea. Given all the things that the mother country used to send out to the colonies in pre-war times, as the fighting in Europe drags on and becomes more extensive, it is the shortages that are now felt the most. It is all well and good having strawberries and raspberries; here, every second person suffers from malaria. Yersin has been taking quinine for thirty years. Each time a ship is torpedoed, its cargo sinks to the bottom of the sea. Indochina's face is already bathed in cold sweat, its hands shake. Then comes the Dardanelles offensive and the malaria epidemic, the troops spewing up their guts into the blue waters of the Sea of Marmara. France reserves its laboratory output for the expeditionary corps of the Army of the East.

Yersin steps into his library and takes down the works of La Condamine, well aware that he is the man's surprise heir. Charles Marie de La Condamine, explorer and man of science like himself, was the first, on returning from his trip down the Amazon, to describe not only the rubber tree but also the cinchona tree. The French Academy of Sciences printed the texts of his *Report on a Recently Discovered Elastic Resin* and his paper *On the Cinchona Tree*. Yersin writes to his friends in Java and has them send him several cinchona plants. He makes the first acclimatisation trials.

The trees will not grow even with upward traction. It takes months for it to occur to anyone that the Hon Ba soil is unsuitable. Yersin obtains a chemical analysis of the Javanese soils in which production flourishes and, armed with annual temperature and rainfall curves, he searches for a region in Annam having comparable statistics. In Russia, the October Revolution breaks out.

The world has seen nothing yet. The century is just limbering up. Seventeen years old and already a serious lout. The cap with the peak upturned and the fag-end dangling from the corner of the mouth, the pistol tucked into the belt. A global war costing millions of lives is followed by civil war raging from Moscow to Vladivostok, famine and the typhus epidemic. Yersin and his little Nha Trang crowd go on germinating their seeds in trays, varying compositions of growing mediums and quantities of added fertiliser. They criss-cross the countryside carrying out core bores and bringing these back to the lab. Their choice falls on Dran Hill, one thousand metres high, over towards Dalat. They know it will all take years – as much time as attaining the proletarian paradise. An even more promising site is found at Djiring, eighty kilometres from Nha Trang.

One evening the radio announces that the date is 11 November and an armistice has been signed. That same day Apollinaire is buried with a shell-hole in his head. Four days later, at his Hon Ba chalet, Yersin takes up pen and Institute-headed notepaper to write: 'Dear Calmette, I am pleased and moved that, after more than four years' separation, I can restore the link between us.'

Communications are re-established and the survivors return to civilian life. Yersin recruits a researcher in plant biology, André Lambert, whose early career was with the Grenoble-based 'Society for Processing Cinchonas'. It is the start of a fifteen-year friendship. The two men share a predilection for a job well done and for hiking in the mountains. They resume the research work, starting to co-sign their publications in the *Review of Applied Botany*.

Yersin places the direction of Indochina's Pasteur Institutes in the hands of his future biographer, Noël Bernard, now back from the war, who will eulogise him in these words: 'There can be few examples of such disinterestedness. He hung back to allow others the freedom of initiative to which he was so passionately attached himself.' Yersin decides to devote himself to the study of quinine. With increasing frequency he seeks out his mountain retreat, spending more and more time alone there. Surrounded by his birdcages and Siamese cats. From the war's end onwards, he again corresponds with Roux and Calmette. These letters, both friendly and scientific, constitute his diary. 'The lab assistant who died was not just anybody: he was a son of the former King of Annam.' The man had inoculated himself with plague by accident. Yersin wants everything recorded in the archives, keen that none of the combatants who fall at the scientific front shall be forgotten. 'His name was Vinh Tham, he was a lad with a very open, intelligent mind.'

In France, behind the old stagers Roux and Calmette, a new generation of Pasteurians is growing up whom Yersin does not know. Bordet receives the Nobel for his work on antibodies. Louis-Ferdinand Destouches (the future Céline) and André Lwoff (the future Nobel laureate) are sent off to Roscoff to study seaweed. Yersin has lost the will to travel. Steamers are still just as slow, and the Trans-Siberian is in the hands of the Red Army. More than thirty years since he first embarked on the *Oxus*, his enthusiasm has gone. 'Those long sea voyages are dreadfully monotonous. If only there were an organised aeroplane service!' He'd have liked to found Air France ten years early, Yersin would.

In the end it is at the request of the Institute that he decides to book a passage. 'The boat that suits me best, the *Porthos*, leaves Saigon on 30 November. That will get me to Paris just in time for the New Year celebrations, which will be a bore because everything will be closed and I'll be wasting time! I shall stay at the Lutetia, as I did the last few times, and if Mr Roux is agreeable I should be pleased to dine with him.'

Before leaving he receives a vet at Nha Trang, one Henri Jacotot, another ex-student on Roux's course, who has come to take charge of training lab assistants and health inspectors. The plantation and stockbreeding facilities are still expanding. Now that shipping is no longer at risk from torpedoes, various breeds of sheep are being imported, Kelantans and Bizets, along with Breton cows and a Savoyard bull, with the aim of boosting pasteurised-milk production. Yersin is an ancient white-bearded shepherd with a long staff leading a flock more than three thousand strong. Now that it is in profit, thanks to rubber and soon quinine, the company invested in by 'Messrs Yersin, Roux and Calmette' has been sold to the Pasteur Institute for a symbolic one franc and is financing research. Ground is still being cleared, because all those animals need feeding. The land is sown with rye-grass, vernal grass and clover.

So there he is, Yersin, permanently in line for some rosette or other from a local agricultural show while another Pasteurian, Charles Nicolle, receives the Nobel for his work on the transmission of typhus.

Vaugirard

This is real winter. Not the fake winter he has contrived for himself at Hon Ba and has ended up believing is a Lausanne winter. This is bloody freezing. They've scattered salt on the pavements. Yersin, a man of over sixty, is dressed in a black overcoat, hat and muffler. Seven years have passed since his last visit to Europe, and he has not worn this outfit once in the meantime, nor donned gloves.

He resumes his strolls through the Paris streets, accompanied by a small cloud of steam: his breath. That is something he had forgotten, it takes him back to his childhood on the shore of the Lake. He smiles, newly hesitant to cross boulevards because of the profusion and speed of motor taxis, they too trailing white plumes of exhaust through the ice-cold air. He thinks of all the money his friend Serpollet trousered. He eyes the tyres, some made of rubber from Suoi Giao. Decorations twinkle in the bare branches of trees. Yersin has heard on the radio of this modernity, this frenzy that is thought to have followed the carnage of the war to end all wars. That whole atmosphere of the Twenties – the 'Crazy Years', they are calling them in France.

The tall iron tower is lit up. He remembers it being erected, then inaugurated, four years after his arrival in Paris that summer when, bowing to orders, he agreed to deliver the microbiology course in Roux's stead. The summer of the centenary of the Revolution. More heavily here than in Nha Trang, he feels on his shoulders the burden of History or simply the burden of his life. He is now the same age as Wigand and Pasteur were when he knew them in Marburg and Paris. He strolls past the place de la Concorde, once the scene of revolution and discord, and on down quai de la Mégisserie to see the animals. It is too cold. The cages have been kept inside.

Never having drawn much of a distinction between himself and the Institute, he now finds the revenues from veterinary vaccines, rubber and quinine piling up. Yersin is a wealthy man. He takes little advantage of the fact. At Vilmorin's, he chooses seeds and bulbs, lilies and begonias, cockscombs and petunias, cyclamens, zinnias, dahlias, Spanish brooms and red poppies. He has one consigment sent to quai des Messageries, Marseilles, and the other to Switzerland, a bouquet for his sister. He returns to the hotel. He knows none of the new regulars at the Lutetia. They include now fashionable writers. André Gide when not in the Congo, and Blaise Cendrars when not in Brazil. The two lift attendants are wounded war veterans with chestfuls of medals. Yersin has not seen Paris for seven years. For seven years he has missed the faces of those dear to him, Calmette and Roux in France, Émilie in Switzerland. Too long. He feels a bit lost.

In the morning he crosses the road in front of the hotel and descends the steps of Sèvres-Babylone station, buys a first-class ticket, and finds line 12 – still, at that time, called 'North–South'. It takes him straight to the Institute. 'In the metro, which I use a lot, the crush is indescribable. The crowds on the boulevards are dense and form an uninterrupted stream. The Pasteur Institute quarter is less busy, one might almost be in the country.' It is down those streets, the quiet streets, that he prefers to stroll. Rue Dutot, rue des Volontaires and the streets crossing them or running parallel to them, rue Mathurin-Régnier, rue Plumet, rue Blomet. Vaugirard municipality was tacked on to Paris under the Second Empire, in the sixtieth year of the previous century, the year when Mouhot came across the temples of Angkor, when Pasteur climbed the Sea of Ice. Twenty-five years later, international subscription made it possible to purchase several hectares of horticultural land there on which to build the Institute, with cabbage fields all around.

Now, in these mid-Twenties, a mere stone's throw from the disinfected white benches, the sterilised syringes and microscopes, the neat, clean laboratories, the gilt and black marble of the Byzantine crypt, the hovels and workshops of Vaugirard have become the studios of artists associated with the Bal nègre cabaret. The new inhabitants of factories abandoned during the war and since relocated farther out in the suburbs and stuffed with workmen from North Africa by crippled industrialists, survivors of the great *poilu* massacre – they are artists who have failed and will doubtless always fail to gain entry to the Lutetia. Unknowns fallen on hard times. Devotees of painting and literature and all that crap. The rue Blomet crowd. Masson, Leiris, Desnos, Miró – the old man in the black overcoat may well have seen some of them at Volontaires metro station, those young men in jackets alighting from second-class carriages. 'Volontaires station and the famous metro entrances reminded me of the great Gaudí, who so influenced me,' the Catalan painter will write when one day he too has become fashionable.

The ghost of the future, the man with the moleskin notebook who has pursued Yersin like his shadow and who likewise disembarked from Nha Trang with frozen feet, accompanies

Yersin on these walks. In rue Plumet, because it really is too cold out, the two push open the door of the Select, a bar in a time warp whose internal layout cannot have changed since the Twenties. They order coffees.

The ghost of the future, having copied a few lines from Robert Desnos into his notebook, now shows them to Yersin.

An idler strolling along rue Blomet one afternoon will see, not far from the Bal nègre cabaret, a large tumbledown building. Grass grows there. The trellised shrubbery of the house next door spills over the wall, and through a lofty carriage entrance a stout tree can be seen. This is number 45, rue Blomet, where I lived for many years and where some of those who were formerly my friends and several of those who are still my friends will remember coming.

The latter were another little crowd – Artaud, Bataille, Breton – and, as our Catalan painter will recall, once fashionable (for a person who has come into fashion likes to recall that there was a time when he or she was not): 'We drank heavily. Those were the days of brandies with water and curaçao mandarins. They came by metro, by the famous North–South line that functioned as a hyphen between the Montmartre of the Surrealists and the retards of Montparnasse.'

Yersin shrugs, takes down his overcoat, puts on his hat. A playground and the fifteenth arrondissement bowls club occupy the place where the studios once were. One of the Catalan's sculptures, *The Moonbird*, has been sited there in memory of Desnos, who died of typhus in Theresienstadt following his deportation to Buchenwald.

The ghost of the future watches the figure huddled in the black overcoat walk away, back up towards rue Dutot, sees him wave to Joseph Meister as he passes the porter's lodge.

After working meetings with Roux as well as with Eugène Wollman, who is studying bacteriophagy in connection with Yersin's bacillus, because all those little bugs are continually gobbling one another up, Yersin makes himself comfortable in the well-heated office belonging to Calmette, 'where I found a corner of a table to catch up with my correspondence'.

Before leaving the capital he lunches with his friend Doumer, who still hasn't had enough of politics. Four of his sons fell on the field of honour. He recently joined the left-wing cartel, and is once again Minister of Finance in the Aristide Briand government. Had he known what awaited him, he too might have opted for his garden, might have bought seeds at Vilmorin's. Or retired to Dalat to live in the Lang Bian Palace, which he had had built.

For his work on acclimatising quinine, Yersin receives the medal of the Society of Commercial Geography, a modest enough gong when Calmette is now a member of the

Academy of Sciences. He has been passed over, Yersin. He belongs to another century. It was thirty years ago that he conquered plague.

Yersinia pestis.

machinery and implements

The time of science and thought is not the same as that of clocks and calendars. He is a historical throwback, Yersin. An Enlightenment encyclopaedist. Before him, La Condamine published on geography, botany, physics, mathematics, medicine and chemistry as the mood took him. Like Pasteur, La Condamine belonged to both the Academy of Sciences and the French Academy. But Voltaire's friend was an Encyclopaedist with a capital E, working alongside Diderot and d'Alembert. Yersin is an all-rounder, poking his finger into every pie: an expert in tropical agronomy and a bacteriologist, an ethnologist and photographer. He has published at the highest level in the fields of microbiology and botany.

Now he is pursuing yet another idea. His timetable freed up by the miracle of peace, which has given him back his colleagues, he sits up on his roof, in his cane chair, staring through his astronomical telescope.

He has entrusted the medical research to Noël Bernard, the veterinary research to Henri Jacotot, the cinchonas to André Lambert, and the overall management, logistics and accounts to Anatole Gallois, a journalist recently laid off from the *Haiphong Times*. They are his new crowd. As for him, he no longer wishes to hear another word about animals. He intends to devote himself heart and soul to meteorology. From Paris he has brought back a Wulf two-strand electrometer. He has to construct huge kites attached by steel cables to winches and capstans. He flies them right up into the clouds, a kilometre high, and the village children clap. His aim: to measure atmospheric electricity and predict storms and typhoons. Calmette and Roux worry about not hearing from him. 'I am sending up kites to take meteorological readings.'

Quite as much as plague in the Middle Ages, certain atmospheric phenomena are a scourge that kills on a massive scale. Drought, frost, hail showers, storms all bring famine and war. In that part of the world, fishermen vanish in sudden tornadoes. To arrive at reliable predictions will be a contribution to peace and prosperity.

Yersin persuades Fichot, a naval hydrographer with a keen interest in astronomy, to come and live near him in Nha Trang. A staircase leads to the roof terrace of the big square house. A dome protects the telescope ordered from Carl Zeiss of Jena and a prismatic astrolabe. The men make nightly observations. Meanwhile, Yersin studies logarithms, and as he progresses in maths he orders reference books. He wants the section of sky that lies above his realm to be annexed to his realm, together with its stars and comets. Dreaming of Kepler and Tycho Brahe, he seeks to be both simultaneously. The man who observes and the man who makes calculations. On earth as in heaven. He does sometimes see what men once believed they saw. He would like to be confused with Vermeer's *Astronomer*, he would like a museum, one day, to mention his name on its letterhead. From microscope to telescope, he becomes aware of the astonishing geometric proximity of the infinitely large and the infinitely small. And we humans float like jellyfish between the two. Yet he keeps his feet firmly on the ground, fills notebooks, advances in mathematical theory, publishes his findings and his celestial considerations in the *Astronomical Bulletin* founded by Henri Poincaré, the forerunner of relativity. Yersin's light still shines. If not a Nobel for medicine, why not a Nobel for physics?

Then the roof timbers spring. Too much load. In any case, Yersin has had enough of astronomy. He has a different idea.

He arranges for the whole lot to be dismantled and left in the yard for the children to play with. They have long since lost interest in the xograph – a daft plaything, it has to be said. As he ages, he grows more and more fond of children. He takes the village children out fishing in his Serpollet steamboat among the islands in the bay. He has brought a projector back from Paris and shows them documentaries and Charlie Chaplin films. The children laugh. Show us another. And then the kites. There's no stopping them. All right, that's enough. He's had another idea. Everybody out. Scram.

He has a wireless telegraphy network installed between Nha Trang, Suoi Giao and Hon Ba. A Signals officer spends some time in each of his three houses, linking the transmitter-receivers and teaching Yersin and his colleagues how to use them. The three terminals will henceforth be able to exchange news and weather forecasts. People take turns donning the headphones. 'Unfortunately we are too far away to be able to listen to the concerts broadcast by various stations in Europe and America.' Yersin buries himself in technical manuals, writing to Calmette: 'My private electrical laboratory is coming together gradually and gives me great delight. I've managed to tape broadcasts from Bordeaux. Things don't work too well yet because of the atmospheric disturbance, which is very bad at this time of year. Still, if there were no problems there'd be no pleasure.'

*

Having got this far, a fool would have planted a flag. He'd have called himself boss, recruited a militia, commissioned a national anthem, run up the colours on his fleet, started minting money. William Walker and his short-lived republics of Lower California and Sonora. Mayréna and his Kingdom of Sedang. James Brooke, Rajah of Sarawak. A platform and a mike. A uniform and dark glasses. A Guide, a Sultan, a Bao Dai. Maybe a Hollywood wife, too. His realm is a damned sight larger than Monaco.

It's a huge improvement, communicating instantly by radio. But from Nha Trang to Suoi Giao and from Suoi Giao to Hon Ba is still a journey of several hours by canoe and horse transport to take up the seed and bring down the harvest. At this time he puts the extent of his domain at twenty thousand hectares, including the mountain within his 'sphere of influence' but not counting the sky above. When the Academy of Sciences awards him a prize for some clever brainwave, he invests the money in building a winding road thirty kilometres long. He becomes a civil engineer. 'Rather than have the work done by contractors I am directing it myself with the help of our Annamite labourers. I shall be giving our road a regular gradient of ten per cent.' Occasionally explosives are needed to break up the rock. 'We use the rubble to build retaining walls for the embankments, for which we are employing the dry-stone method.' He finishes his letter to

Roux with these words: 'That way the work will cost less and benefit our staff instead of fattening middlemen who use unpaid labour. For the line, I am using a very practical British-made construction tool called Improver Road Tracer.'

The road makes it possible to haul a powerful generating set up to the chalet in order to install lighting to keep the budgerigars entertained and to operate a hydraulic ram that will water the plots and rose bushes. From France, Yersin orders a Citroën half-track vehicle – the same as 'the ones that crossed the Sahara'. Because without giving that impression, without even deliberately pursuing it, the king of rubber and quinine has a keen eye for profit. Yersin the ascetic, entirely on his own initiative, has carved out an empire within the Empire.

Still, if he did win the Nobel he'd go and build himself a little airport.

the king of quinine

The cinchonas are fifteen years old now and in full production. The century is thirty, Yersin sixty-seven. The annual quinine output is several tons. As with rubber, the controlling variants are climatic and zoological. 'Just now we have a large herd of wild elephants at Suoi Giao giving us a lot of trouble, damaging the road and destroying the telephone connection.'

That year, 1930, an unknown revolutionary who has changed his name several times (the current one being Ho Chi Minh), and who ten years earlier attended the Tours Congress at which what later became the French Communist Party was set up, secretly founds the Communist Party of

Indochina. In the days when his name was Nguyen Ai Quoc he studied in France and spent some time in London and Le Havre. He had been a cook on the steamships, and Yersin may have come across him on one of his voyages. He already has the delicate bamboo-like grace and the radiant smile but not yet the little Trotsky beard. Yersin never gives a moment's credence to the revolutionary chorus. Killing men to give life to dreams. Not like young Rimbaud, author of a *Projected Communist Constitution* fifty years before Tours. Which ought to have earned him, posthumously, Party card no. 0. In that same year, 1930, social traitor Doumer is President of the Senate. The Pasteurian Boëz accidentally injects himself with typhoid fever, falls asleep permanently in Dalat. In the pages of the *Records of the Indochinese Pasteur Institutes*, Boëz joins the other combatants who have laid down their lives on the bacteriological front.

The following year sees the Colonial Exhibition in Paris, organised under the patronage of old Lyautey. A replica Angkor Wat is built in the Bois de Vincennes. Yersin and Lambert do not make the journey but mark the occasion by publishing a brochure about cultivating cinchona trees – again, written in the style of Char's 'useful poetry':

The action of phosphoric acid, soluble only with difficulty, and of Tonkin phosphates is not obvious. Potassium in the form of Alsace salts works only weakly, lime appears to have done no good at all, despite the soil being low in this element. Cyanamide and lime nitrate both have a markedly injurious effect, several plants of this series dying and the rest, though developing, doing so rather more slowly than those of other series.

The language is almost as brisk as a line by Cendrars – in itself a potential biography of Yersin: *Gong tom-tom Zanzibar jungle beast X-ray express bistoury.*

Then Lambert passes away at the age of forty-six. All around Yersin, they are starting to drop like flies. He writes his friend's obituary for the *Records*. Friendship is the only paradoxically rational feeling that is not a passion. Yersin, deeply affected, recalls being 'bowled over by the qualities of this work colleague and friend'. A portrait of a friend is invariably a self-portrait, attributing to the friend the virtues one would like to see in the mirror. 'A man of character and conscience, he bestowed his friendship only advisedly but, having once done so, stayed loyal to that friendship with a quiet firmness and complete dedication.'

Because at the end of the day, one may or may not have a vaccine against plague but never, as one knows full well, will a vaccine be found against the death of friends, there is no sense in thinking that it will. A man may pride himself on exemplary success. Or may not. The walls of Yersin's mind have been proof against passion since boyhood. Stainless steel. Never will the reactor's core break through the protective shield, otherwise the least little crack can bring catastrophe, explosion, annihilation, depression, melancholy (worse: literature and painting and all that crap) or a string of scientific fads. It can cause such pressure on the valve that the sporadic jet of thought, moving round and round, sprays everywhere, multiplying inventions in all domains. And no doubt Yersin scarcely cares, himself, whether or not his name tops the bill. No doubt he does it all because there is no gilding the lily.

The world is poised at the top of the toboggan run, about to go hurtling down into the Second World War. Yersin sends work back to France that he does not know is the new Futurist poetry, work like his *Observations on Atmospheric Electricity in Indochina*, published by the Academy of Sciences. Doumer is elected President of the Republic. Yersin, up at Hon Ba, continues to keep his distance. The world moves on behind his back. He takes no interest. All that filth of History and Politics, he thinks he can ignore it for ever. Were he to read Baudelaire, he would embrace the man's individualism: there can be no real progress save in and through the individual. Yersin is a loner. He knows that nothing great has ever been achieved by the multitude. He hates groups, rating their intelligence as being in inverse proportion to the number of members making them up. Genius always stands alone. The committee has the lucidity of the hamster. The stadium the perspicacity of the paramecium.

One evening the radio announces that Doumer has been shot by Russian medic Pavel Gorguloff – either a madman or a Fascist, we shall never really know.

Doumer had writer friends: Pierre Loti dedicated his *An Angkor Pilgrim* to him. On the day of the assassination, a friend of Loti's, Claude Farrère, was standing near the President. Like Loti, Farrère was once a sailor on the Bosphorus, Farrère the Academician, winner of the Goncourt before the war for his *Les Civilisés*, a novel set in Saigon. Farrère also, the radio says, took a slug in the belly during the tussle that followed the shooting but is expected to recover. Years back, Yersin remembers, Doumer and he were a team climbing the foothills leading to Lang Bian Plateau, the then future site of Dalat. He also recalls their ascending the Mekong from Saigon to Phnom Penh together, the orphan from Morges and the orphan from Aurillac.

In Aurillac, fifty years before this, the local sheep farmers invite Pasteur to a thank-you party for ridding them of anthrax. They present him with a large carved cup bearing two symbols: microscope and syringe. In the shade of bunting-bedecked plane trees, backed by the town band drawn up in lines and a number of sheep that had won prizes at the agricultural show, the mayor stands up and addresses the black-frockcoated figure with the bow tie and blue eyes: 'It's quite small, our Aurillac, and you won't find here the brilliant throngs that inhabit big cities, but you will find minds capable of sensing your kindness and holding it in memory.' Among the listeners is orphan Doumer, then a young maths teacher. And he does indeed hold that kindness in memory – to the point of founding the Hanoi health complex twenty years later and putting Pasteurian Alexandre Yersin in charge.

In the same year, '32, that saw Doumer's assassination, Émilie dies in Switzerland, surrounded by her poultry cages, and the correspondence between her and her brother comes to an end. It is also in '32 that a former Pasteurian doctor, a renegade Pasteurian turned writer – novelist, to be precise – publishes his *Journey to the End of Night*.

Alexandre & Louis

At eighteen, this son of a passage Choiseul lacemaker signs up for three years. He is put in the 12th Armoured Cavalry, then stationed in Rambouillet, where he rises to the modest rank of sergeant. It is bed and board, of course, but a bad idea, as it turns out. The year '14 is not long in coming. However, hey presto, at twenty he sustains the war wound that earns him initially a Military Medal and his portrait on the cover of an illustrated magazine, subsequently his discharge as a seventy-five per cent invalid. At least he will never see Verdun. The Anglophile hero is dispatched to Britain. From Britain he goes to Cameroon, from which the Germans have been ousted, becomes an adventurer for the Oubangui-Sangha Company, makes a three-week march to Bikobimbo, and there falls ill with malaria and dysentery.

Louis-Ferdinand Destouches finds in Africa what Yersin found in Asia and described in a letter to Fanny: 'The sort of wild freedom one enjoys here passes all understanding in Europe, where everything is so regulated by civilisation.'

Europe, in both cases, will lose them.

After the war, in the early Twenties, the future Céline, now a medical student, obtains a placement at the Pasteur Institute. He is sent to study seaweed and bacteria in Roscoff, together with the young André Lwoff, then aged eighteen. Louis-Ferdinand Destouches is writing his thesis on Ignaz Semmelweiss, a Hungarian medical hygienist, Pasteurian before his time, a misunderstood genius, committed to a mental hospital where, a rebel, he dies at the hands of staff. Because genius is like that: no middle way, the gilt and marble of the Panthéon or the straitjacket, there is so little between them. In his thesis, writing as a good Pasteurian, Céline pays homage to the frockcoat and bow tie: 'Fifty years later Pasteur, shining a more powerful light, was to illuminate the microbial truth in a way that was irrefutable and complete.'

He becomes a medical hygienist with the League of Nations in Geneva, performing various missions in the United States, Canada and Cuba. He may, for a while, have dreamt of a scientific career, a Nobel Prize, before chucking the idea. Instead, he puts a bomb under the novel as Rimbaud put a bomb under poetry. He opens a surgery in the suburbs of Paris, devotes evenings to his scribbling, deaf to any more talk of medical research. And one thinks of Yersin at the time of Calmette's and Loir's incessant solicitations: 'And what's more, it is my very firm intention not to return to the Pasteur Institute.'

In Céline's novel, Louis Pasteur becomes Bioduret Joseph. A suburban GP, back from the blood and mud and barbed-wire entanglements of war, is living the life of the poor, which is the same before and after victory, before the monuments and flags and the lies of politics and after. A child, Bébert, lies at death's door. 'Around the seventeenth day I did in fact tell myself that I'd better go and ask them at the Bioduret Joseph Institute what they thought of a case of typhoid like this.'

The description of the Institute is terrible. The suburban doctor tells us of the shambles and stench as the lab assistants, taking advantage of the free gas supply, slow-cook their pots of stew amid 'tiny cadavers of disembowelled animals, fag-ends, dented gaslamps, cages and jars, the latter with mice in them, slowly suffocating'. The Pasteurians may have cried scandal and protested at treason, but one also recalls Yersin's words: 'The laboratory existence one led there became impossible, it seems to me, once one had tasted freedom and the life of the open air.'

The GP tracks down the elderly, disillusioned scientist

Parapine, his teacher back in the days when he believed. In that black overcoat with the collapsed shoulders now covered in dandruff, his white moustache now stained yellow by tobacco, Parapine pokes fun at his middle-aged, high-minded lab assistant, his 'boy'. 'My slightest antic thrills him. Wasn't it ever thus, eh, whatever the religion? Surely since time immemorial the priest's thoughts have always been far from the Good Lord while his beadle stays true to the faith … Iron belief, they call it. Makes you sick, it really does.'

Yersin: 'Scientific research is very interesting, but Mr Pasteur was quite right when he said that, unless he is a genius, a man must be wealthy to work in a laboratory and risk leading a miserable existence, even if it does win him a certain scientific renown.'

Céline: 'It's because of this Bioduret that for the last half-century so many young people have gone into scientific research. Laboratories have wasted as many lives as the Conservatoire. With the result, eventually, that such incompetents all begin to look alike, after a certain number of years of failing to make it.'

The troubled young doctor visits 'the tomb of the great scientist Bioduret Joseph, located in the very cellars of the Institute amid all the gold and marble. A bourgeois-Byzantine fantasy in the most exalted taste.' The crypt and the mosaics that old Joseph Meister, eight years after the novel appears, as those Germans walk into the Pasteur Institute, has no wish to see defiled.

Whatever enters the old man's mind before that final bullet? Whyever did he bring that old gun back from the '14–'18 war? And why, for the past twenty years, has he kept it cleaned and greased, wrapped in a rag and concealed at the back of a drawer? No doubt he thinks the weapon goes with his job as concierge, as keeper of the temple, a last bastion. Perhaps, being from Alsace, he is aware that victory is always provisional and that one day the enemy will be back. That he ought to be keeping better watch over the mortal remains of a man who has been dead for forty-five years. The Germans guffaw at an old man seeking to bar their way, as if he, on his own, feels more impenetrable than the entire Maginot Line. They jostle him, thrust him aside. They descend the stairs towards the gold and marble. The little old man flees. Does he see the dog again, the fangs, the white froth dripping from its jaws? A shot rings out. The safety catches of sub-machine guns click back, orders are barked, the intruders run back up the stairs. They learn that the old man now lying in a pool of blood had but one mission in life: to be the first person saved from rabies. The proof of Pasteur's theory. A guinea pig.

almost a dwem

For years, Bernard and Jacotot keep the business going, developing vaccine sales and opening kennels for dog rabies and pigsties for swine fever. It has long since moved on from being a craft-trade to an industry proper. The thousand shots of pre-'14 are more than one hundred thousand now. The members of the medical team are Nha Trang trained, experimenter Bui Quang Phuong will remain there for twenty-five years, as will lab assistants Le Van Da and Ngo Dai and their colleagues. The latter are still young and like all of us have no notion of the future. They will already be dotards at the time of the Indochina wars.

Because the world, in '32, has seen nothing yet. The First

War was practice. Even Russia on fire and bleeding from Moscow to Vladivostok was nothing. One day the century turns thirty-three. The age at which Christ and Alexander the Great died. Centuries, however, are fated to live to a hundred. The little lout grows up to be the ringleader. In Berlin a couple of art collectors, Hitler and Goering, come to power, and in Paris, that same year, Calmette and Roux die within two weeks of each other.

Roux, like Pasteur, merits national obsequies. He is buried in the courtyard of the Institute. The last to be buried there. Otherwise, future generations will be unable to reach their labs without walking over the remains of scientists. His name is given to the section of rue Dutot that joins up with Boulevard Pasteur. In Céline's novel, Roux is Jaunisset, and Parapine 'described the famous Jaunisset to me in seconds as a forger, a maniac of the most fearful kind, and went on to accuse him of more monstrous, hidden, secret crimes than it would take to fill a whole penal colony for a hundred years'. Yersin: 'In the world of academia there is more jealousy, bad faith and disappointment than perhaps anywhere else.'

After the deaths of Calmette and Roux, Yersin is the last surviving member of the Pasteurian crowd, a position he will fill for ten years. He becomes an honorary director of the mother house. Each year he leaves Saigon by Air France, puts up at the Lutetia and chairs the organisation's council at the Holy See, presiding over the assembled directors of the Pasteur Institutes of Casablanca and Tananarive, Algiers and Teheran, Istanbul and elsewhere, himself representing those of Hanoi, Dalat and Saigon, as well as the associate laboratories of Hue, Phnom Penh and Vientiane.

Since the last session of May '40 and his final return aboard the little white whale made of anodised Duralumin, Yersin has tried to keep in touch by radio from the big square house, headset over his ears. The year is now '43. With an Axis victory, the Pasteur Institutes will disappear, of course – or else become Koch or Kitasato Institutes.

However, last year the Allies landed in North Africa. Things are starting to look bad for the Germans and the Japanese. At this crucial moment, with the war at a turning-point, Pasteurian Eugène Wollman, the one we met working on the bacteriophages that attack the Yersin bacillus, who like all the Institute's Jews has been advised to leave Paris for the free zone while it still exists – and has refused – is arrested at the Institute by the French police and sent with his wife to Drancy. He will die in Auschwitz. The future heroes and Nobel laureates for bacteriology have joined the Resistance. André Lwoff's team secretly produce vaccines for *maquisards*. Yersin, of course, knows nothing of all this. For more than three years he paces to and fro. He is nearly eighty now, waiting for the end, his own or that of the war, waiting on the veranda of the big square house beside the sea, seated in his rocking chair.

For ten years now, Calmette has been a dwem. Roux, too, has become a dwem. For a long time, ever since his discovery of the word 'posh' (now all the rage on the steamships), Yersin has been acquainted with the habit of the English language of forming words with initial letters. This one, though, 'dwem', is American and lumps together British, French, Germans and Italians: *dead white European males*. Not just Roux and Calmette but also Dante and da Vinci, Pasteur and Wollman, Pascal, Goethe and Beethoven, Marat, Cook, Garibaldi, Rimbaud, Cervantes, Magellan, Galileo and Euclid, Shakespeare and Chateaubriand. All the people who until recently were called great, now transfixed like insect varieties, dwems mounted on card with wing cases spread, a useless, slightly quaint collection from days of yore. Yersin writes his will.

Both Roux and Pasteur revered the Republic and its triple motto. And the fact that none of the three words means anything without the others. Liberty is not licence, nor can the unjust man know liberty, being a slave to his passions. Equality must be equality of opportunity from the start and equal respect for merit at the end. In consequence, inheritance is banned except in so far as the emotions are concerned, ergo small beer. The bulk should go to the community.

I bequeath to the Pasteur Institute of Indochina, which will dispose of them as it sees fit, the buildings I have had erected, all my furniture, my refrigerator, radio receiver, cameras, together with my entire library and all my scientific apparatus. The appliances relating to physical geography, astronomy, meteorology, etc. may be given to the Phu-Lien Central Observatory should no one at the Pasteur Institute be in a position to make use of them. I desire that my aged, faithful Annamite servants be granted life pensions from the interest on a long-term bond that I took out for this purpose from the Hong Kong Shanghai Bank in Saigon and that is held by Mr Gallois at Suoi Giao. I ask Mr Jacotot to be so good as to take charge of distributing these pensions among the following servants: Nuoi, Dung and Xe primarily, then to my gardener Trinh-Chi, to Du who looks after my birds, to Chutt, and to everyone in my household whom Mr Jacotot deems worthy thereof.

The envelope is sealed and delivered to Jacotot, accompanied by a short letter in which Yersin asks for a small Vietnamese ceremony with incense and a meal on the fiftieth day, with white flags. Votive notes are to be burnt, and the deceased's altar furnished with a bowl of rice, a hard-boiled egg, a cooked chicken and a bunch of bananas. He wishes to be buried at Suoi Giao, midway between Nha Trang and Hon

Ba, at the centre of the world and of the estate. Now everything is in order. He has selected the site and marked it out, chosing to reduce his realm from several tens of thousands of hectares to two square metres.

So there he sits, Yersin, waiting amid all this beauty. A genius and possibly, at bottom, a nutcase. There is so little in it. A genius who will meet a more peaceful end than Semmelweiss. Yet one imagines that, had fate confined him to a psychiatric hospital, he too would have rebelled. He has tried to shut himself up in his own lazaret, a garden cut off from the world, from viruses and politics and sex and war, tried to isolate himself in a forty-year quarantine where he can pursue his fads. A fall might have followed such presumption. It has often happened. A storybook ending of some kind, a murder, a sudden new development, something sublime, or possibly ridiculous, a petty theft. Yersin downsliding into kleptomania or alcoholism. But no, Yersin does not stumble. Yet from start to finish he remains human.

Surrounded by so many lives, so much chaos, the life of Yersin is quite as good as the next person's. Here is a man of reason who never lets his feelings run away with him. A man of the Greek Enlightenment, and of the four pillars he has opted for the Portico and the Garden over the Lyceum and the Academy. From his last trip (no one knows this) he has brought back the Classics. At night, in the big square house, spectacles before weary blue eyes, Yersin turns the pages of texts in Greek and Latin, covering up the translation and writing his own in pencil. It is the last secret, the final enigma. He has only to die to become a dwem in his turn. He lacks only the first initial.

on the veranda

It is solidly built, the big square house with the arcades, he made sure of that. Big enough for all the fishermen of Xom Con and their families to shelter in on typhoon nights, big enough to accommodate the children who come there to read the illustrated magazines brought back for them from Paris. Yersin waits. He well knows he is about to die, but death is delaying its arrival. He will have lived from the Second Empire to the Second World War. A man's life is History's unit of measurement. The Japs have not reached Nha Trang yet. This is a race between death and the Japanese. Now he is a Julien Gracq character. He keeps watch out to sea, from which the enemy may come.

There is still fighting in Europe, and now, in these parts, it is the Pacific war. The Americans use every resource. They are funding Ho Chi Minh's Vietminh, who are engaging the occupier in Tonkin. First things first. They intend to see to the French later. In various underground movements, Vietnamese Stalinists and Trotskyites are slaughtering one another. The little Nha Trang crowd is in the thick of it. Each evening, after tidying and cleaning their laboratory benches, Jacotot and Bernard come out to find the old master on the veranda.

Sometimes they are joined by the young writer, Cung Giu Nguyen. He will die in the following century, having reached the age of a hundred, having seen Indochina's three wars – against the French, against the Americans and against the Khmer Rouge. He lived so long that he even saw Communist capitalism, which was something Ho Chi Minh had never imagined. Those evening conversations are held in French. Yersin speaks a purely practical, unnuanced Vietnamese, one that works. Nguyen Phuoc Quynh, before becoming a journalist, was one of those fishermen's children who played in and had the run of the big square house. The latter recalls that 'a feature of the way he used Vietnamese was that he often employed the words *nguoi ta* ("one") for all three persons singular as well as plural, and his "one" applied both to people and to animals'.

They have the sea before them as they sit and talk, flowers and birdcages all around them. The pirate parrot and the

---

sound of breaking waves. Jacotot and Bernard take notes. They have both, independently, decided to write a *Life of Yersin*. His mother and sister are both long gone. Fanny's Fig Tree House has been sold, as has Émilie's chalet, Émilie having died childless. By now, there is probably no trace of him left in Europe. Maybe no trace of Europe will survive, full stop. That year the world is still wondering which side will reach the atom bomb first. Oppenheimer for the Americans or Heisenberg for the Germans. Maybe only Asia will be spared. How, at that time, could anyone have foreseen that another Pasteurian, Mollaret, would one day find all those letters, so carefully preserved, and place them in the archives of the Pasteur Institute?

Yersin is convinced that all his letters to Fanny and his letters to Émilie, which constitute the true record of his life, vanished long ago. So he answers their questions. How he discovered the bacillus and conquered plague. Left Switzerland for Germany, the Pasteur Institute for the steamship line Messageries Maritimes, quit medicine for ethnology and ethnology for agriculture and arboriculture. How in Indochina he became a bacteriological adventurer, then an explorer and cartographer. How he spent two years roaming around in Moi country before penetrating that of the Sedang. The two scientists ask him about his fads and inventions, about horticulture and stockbreeding, mechanics and physics, electricity and astronomy, aviation and photography. How he

---

became king of rubber and king of quinine. How he walked from Nha Trang to the Mekong and ascended that river to Phnom Penh to end up living for fifty years in this village beside the South China Sea. The two scientists fill their notebooks. They look into Yersin's blue eyes – that once looked into the blue eyes of Louis Pasteur.

The ghost of the future watches the old man as he sits in his rocking chair, from the pale gold of morning through to the brass and copper of evening. In the ancient contentment of his days. Yersin well knows he will never again make the climb to the Hon Ba chalet or the farm at Suoi Giao. He sees in imagination the slow pace of the grazing herds. The even slower growth of his vegetables, flowers and fruit. He who knows what men and women are like inside those bags of skin, there he sits, facing the sea and the horizon, aware that his cells are disappearing, or replicating themselves less and less fast, with more and more errors or interference in the message of the (as yet unknown) desoxyribonucleic acid. We do know, however, and have known since Pasteur that nothing is born of nothing and that everything that lives must die. He breathes in the 'smell of last night's leisure feasted', lets the wind bathe his bare head.

Never a Plutarch man, Yersin has not tried to leave his mark on History. Unlike the *Lives* that the Graeco-Roman examined in parallel, biographies of traitors and heroes, Yersin's life offers no example to be shunned or reproduced, no conduct to imitate. Here is a man who has always steered his craft on a solitary course – and done so rather well. Behind him the sea effaces his wake. At nightfall he is helped back to his desk, where he resumes his studies of Greek and Latin.

the ghost of the future

In Yersin's day it was a long way off, Nha Trang. People meant it was a long way from Europe. Nowadays it is at the centre of the world. On the shore of the Pacific, which has succeeded the Atlantic, which succeeded the Mediterranean. Mexico is opposite. Acapulco. It is Europe that is a long way off. On the far side of the earth, the hidden face of the planet. In Dalat, it seems, time stands still on the peaceful waters of the Lake and in the lounges of the Lang Bian Palace, but Nha Trang is absolutely modern.

Yersin would feel less like a fish out of water if he found himself back in Paris today, and were shown into his old room at the Lutetia.

Here, the ghost of the future who has been following him round the world might put up at the Yasaka, on the corner of Yersin Street and the boulevard lining the shore, a glass tower of a hotel that would look quite at home in Bangkok or Miami – wherever, in fact, not the bourgeois mailboat but the equally bourgeois airline sets us down. Nha Trang is a seaside resort frequented mainly by Russians and former North Vietnamese. The large US military base of Cam Ranh, thirty kilometres away, became a Soviet base after Reunification. The only international flight to Nha Trang is from Moscow. Russians fly in to enjoy the twin delights of a tropical climate and the nostalgic hammers and sickles on the red flags lining the beach. At the Yasaka restaurant, the menus are in three languages: Vietnamese, English and Russian. However, in the toilets it is only in English (valiant attempt to force the Russians into multilingualism or subtle joke at the expense of the one-time Big Brother?) that guests are warned not to drink the tapwater.

Where Yersin Street crosses Pasteur Street, in this month of February 2012, construction workers toil day and night on the site of the Nha Trang Palace. The ghost makes for the nearby Pasteur Institute. When the big square house at Fishermen's Point was pulled down several years ago, its entire remaining contents, from the astronomical telescope to the meteorological equipment, were transferred to an annexe of the Institute, where a small Yersin Museum opened. There the visitor will find a reconstruction of his study. The room itself is in dark wood, the already antiquated scientific instruments of copper or bronze. The ghost of the future sits in Yersin's rocking chair. On the walls he identifies maps of the man's expeditions. On a table, his book about the Moi. *Montagnards*, they are called in French, 'mountain dwellers', a generic term that has gone out of use. Nowadays we prefer to speak of 'ethnic minorities'. In the Dalat region, the Lat, the Chill, the Sre. Around Suoi Dau, the Jaglai.

On the shelves, hundreds of works in French and German, dealing with his fads. History books. However, this library may also include books from the collections of other early Pasteurians at Nha Trang: Bernard, Jacotot – Gallois, possibly. Did Yersin read that book up there by Alain Gerbault, the solo circumnavigator?

On his desk, Virgil poems typed out in Latin, double-spaced, with a line-by-line translation pencilled in the spaces. Lists of Vietnamese sentences to memorise. A photograph of him in Paris with film-maker Louis Lumière. His last airline ticket, dated 30 May 1940. Yersin certainly had the best seat of the twelve, seat K – on its own, ranged left, at the rear of the aeroplane. The ticket lists the drinks available to passengers, the brands of whisky, cognac and champagne that the monied émigrés must have downed merrily before the last Air France flight took off from Paris under the noses of the Germans. Another photograph of him on his final return in June '40, alighting from the little white whale in Saigon.

From here a person can extend the walk northward by three hundred metres, heading in the direction of the river. Where the big square house with the arcades once stood there is now a rest home for deserving policemen from all corners of the Socialist Republic of Vietnam. The open-air Svetlana restaurant, down on a level with the noisy rollers, is closed for the off-season. The caretaker agrees to let a stranger shelter from the fine rain – but who will say 'no' to a ghost? This one takes a seat amid the din of the waves. Only the view towards the horizon is unchanged.

The fishermen have been deported to a fresh village across the river to make way for the hotels. In a dilapidated café backing onto the bridge, a café that serves only two drinks, tea or coffee, five dwem portraits are affixed to the wall in a slightly incongruous arrangement: Bach, Beethoven, Einstein, Balzac and Bonaparte. No Yersin, no Pasteur. Yet the latter are both venerated in Vietnam and their names crop up repeatedly at street corners. Pasteur is a saint of the Cao Dai religion, which is chiefly practised in the Mekong delta. Yersin is a Bodhisattva in the pagoda in Suoi Cat, not far from here. Seated on a plastic chair at the edge of the pavement, the ghost watches the constant stream of cars and mopeds crossing the bridge over the river. Yersin was the first to bring a car here. The first to photograph this splendid bay.

From what was once Fishermen's Point but today, as Xom Con, has no fishermen, reaching Hon Ba entails crossing the city, turning north on Mandarin Road in the direction of Hanoi, then taking a right-hand exit and heading into the mountains, negotiating thirty kilometres of hairpin bends. Ethnic minorities burn and clear the foothills, producing timber – eucalyptus and acacia – and cashew nuts. Banana plantations, maize, tall grasses with sharp-edged blades. In front of bamboo hovels, hens scratch and calves, frightened by the engine, bolt. After an hour's drive, a red-and-white police barrier and a guard hut. Beyond, rockfalls and landslides are frequent occurrences in this rainy season. Higher up, one might think one was in familiar jungle, in Honduras or El Salvador, and from then on the temperature drops with each hairpin bend, the sky clouds over, mist descends. The excursion seems endless, but suddenly the barking of dogs is heard through the fog and the road terminates in a large pool of muddy water.

Four men live up here, far from everything: two looking after Yersin's reconstructed chalet and, in a latticework cabin on a mound opposite, two forest wardens. A hundred-year-old tea plant between the buildings. The chalet contains a few pieces of furniture made of dark wood, one of them Yersin's bed, some scientific equipment, an ancient suitcase in a wardrobe. Clouds swirl in like cigarette smoke through open windows and doors. Everything is damp, dripping, as if freshly painted. Out in the forest with its huge ferns, beneath the rain, the watchmen find traces of former stables, drinking troughs, rocks that were hollowed out to form seed trays for the first cinchona plants. Large brown lizards put up by the dogs leap into trees. Down below, a foaming stream, yellow with alluvium. Later, sitting over hot tea in the soaking-wet chalet, they pick leeches off my legs; as if the foolish worms imagined they could feed off the blood of a ghost.

Halfway back to Nha Trang, at Suoi Giao, now called Suoi Dau, a blue-painted gate leads into a field. The gate is padlocked. A telephone number to summon the keeper. Beyond the gate, a shepherd in a conical hat, wielding a long staff, leads a flock of sheep, accompanied by large white birds. The track to the experimental farm is lined with flowering lantanas, sugar cane, tobacco and budding rice. Then up a steep path beside which labourers metaphorically wield scythes. The sky-blue tomb sits atop a hillock. No sign of religious obedience. Just this inscription, in capitals:

ALEXANDRE YERSIN

1863–1943

On the left, a tiny orange and yellow pagoda bristles with incense sticks. The two sky-blue metres of Vietnamese territory that were once the centre of this realm. Here Yersin found rest, found his place and his inscription. A *Life of Yersin* might be written as a *Life of St X*. An anchorite who, living in seclusion in a chalet in the chill jungle, kicks over every social constraint to lead the life of a hermit, a grumpy old man, a savage, an original genius, a splendid crank.

the little crowd

Instead of his life, he would no doubt have preferred one to write something along these lines. The little crowd gathered around science personified, the tall silhouette in the black frockcoat and bow tie. The little crowd then dispersing to pasteurise the world and rid it of germs. Many are orphans or stateless persons who, in choosing a father, find they have also chosen a fatherland. They are daredevils, too, adventurers, because in that day and age there is as much danger in getting close to infectious diseases as in taking off in an aircraft made of wood. A crowd of loners. Wild shouting matches and unshakeable friendships. The tiny group of activists behind the bacterial revolution.

The volcano explodes in Paris, these are the glowing coals that fall at random in deserts and forests. Brave young men who buckle their trunkfuls of test tubes, autoclaves and microscopes, board trains and steamers, descend on outbreaks of disease. There is a chivalrous quality to their exploits, and there is something pastoral in their Pasteurian mission. Wielding syringes like swords, these rootless hidalgos, exiles, provincials, foreigners depart for the four corners of the earth. Roux, the orphan from Confolens, runs things from his base in the French capital, centralising discoveries. It is a brotherhood. The Pasteur crowd in universal competition with the Koch crowd, which must be wiped off the board without delay. There are still blank areas on the map and unknown diseases. Everything is still possible, and the medical world is quite new.

It will not last, of that they are aware. They are on the spot at the right time to have their name in Latin attached to that of a bacillus. They practise the Pasteurian method, as perfected with rabies. Take samples, identify, cultivate the virus, then dilute to obtain the vaccine. They stand to benefit from the acceleration of means of transport – steam, for instance, which enables them to be on site as soon as an epidemic appears. Within years, scourges are floored like Homeric monsters, one after another – leprosy, typhoid fever, malaria, tuberculosis, cholera, diphtheria, tetanus, typhus, plague.

*

Not a few of them meet their own deaths in the process. Roux travels to Egypt to study cholera, accompanied by Louis Thullier. Thullier, with a first in physics, back from a vaccination programme in Russia. At twenty-six, he is already the discoverer of the bacillus that causes swine erysipelas or diamond skin disease and has co-signed, with Roux, Pasteur and Chamberland, a paper entitled 'New facts serving to identify rabies'. The moment he sets foot in Egypt he contracts cholera and dies. Sedan is a long way off here, so is politics. A truce reigns. The two teams fraternise. According to Roux, in a letter dispatched to Pasteur immediately: 'Mr Koch and his colleagues arrived as soon as word got around. They found the nicest things to say about our dear departed.' And before describing the cholera bacillus (because this time it is he who wins), 'Mr Koch held one of the corners of the pall. We embalmed our comrade. He lies in a sealed zinc coffin.' Rest in peace, comrade. You will be reunited with Pesas and Vinh Tham, both of whom died of plague in Nha Trang, and with Boëz, who passed on in Dalat.

Following Pasteur's death, the little crowd of lay apostles swarms out over every continent, opening Institutes, disseminating science and reason. They write to one another constantly from opposite ends of the earth, wherever and whenever liners leave port. Their letters, written at a sitting in fountain pen, use the Positivist language of the Third Republic, couched in impeccable syntax. Perhaps not Michelets to a man, the correspondents are Quinets at least. Cultured scientists, aware that certain French words – *amour*, *délice*, *orgue* – become feminine in the plural. Like sailors, they cite their present position. Calmette in Algiers, then in Saigon, then in Lille. Carougeau leaving Nha Trang for Tananarive. Loir, after Sydney, sets up the Tunis Pasteur Institute and studies rabies in Rhodesia, after which he embarks for Montreal to teach biology. Nicolle is in Istanbul, where Remlinger succeeds him before moving on to Tangier. Haffkine, the Jew from Ukraine, opens a laboratory in Calcutta. Wollman, the Jew from Byelorussia, is sent out to Chile. After several years in Guiana, Simond winds up the plague story in Karachi before leaving to study yellow fever in Brazil.

In Nha Trang, telegrams notify Yersin of the deaths of all his old friends and the scattering of the younger survivors. Like Roux, he has no descendants, or only mythical ones. The orphans of Confolens and Morges having adopted Pasteur as their spiritual father, their sons will be spiritual too. Their lab assistants become researchers in their turn. Yersin has grown too old in a world that is no longer his. Louis Pasteur's last living collaborator. He will not write his memoirs. This book would not have pleased him. What am I poking my nose into now?

No doubt it is the chain that should be described rather than the links. A chain measuring a century and a half in length. Pasteur picks Mechnikov who picks Wollman, Eugène Wollman who, on his return from Chile, works on the bacteriophages of Yersin's bacillus before being deported to Auschwitz, while his son joins the Resistance. After the war the son, Élie Wollman, is picked by André Lwoff and in his laboratory works alongside François Jacob, who joined the Free French forces in London and fought from Libya to Normandy. The pair take up the work that Eugène Wollman was doing. Jacob shares the Nobel with Lwoff and Monod. Monod, together with Paul-Émile Victor, explores Greenland in the Thirties before joining the Resistance. Twenty years after his Nobel, Lwoff writes his article 'Louis-Ferdinand Céline and scientific research' – because in any activist core, whatever a person does, be it trying to get right away like Yersin or saying bad things like Céline, traducing then becoming part of literature, there is no escaping the attention of the little crowd.

It is the final enigma of Yersin's life, literature. Only after his death, when his records are sorted out, is it uncovered. He dips into literature, and he too becomes addicted. He learns what Rimbaud meant by his 'it means nothing'. Rimbaud begins with Latin, Latin is where Yersin ends up. This final addiction is more powerful than cocaine – his one vice.

It is Jacotot who discovers Yersin's clandestine translation workshop while tidying his desk. The sheets of paper and books with, on their bindings, the telltale owl or she-wolf. At age eighty he goes back to studying Latin and Greek, covering up the left-hand page. Translating is like writing a Life. Invention held in check, the paradoxical freedom of the violin playing a score, the bow-strokes, the weightless leaps up the E-string, the muted rhythm of the low notes. A stunned Jacotot piously compiles the bibliography: Phaedrus, Virgil, Horace, Sallust, Cicero, Plato, Demosthenes. Probably Yersin finds in their works the classical values that are his own: simplicity and rectitude, serenity and moderation. In the end, he comes to love literature; solitude he had always loved.

the sea

From time to time the old injuries from the fight with Thouk give him trouble, the spear thrust between the ribs and the split thumb. His legs no longer bear his weight. He is sitting in his rocking chair. Not that that means he is idle, necessarily. In the deepest part of his aged brain Pasteur's words echo like an injunction: 'It would seem to me I were committing a theft if I let a day pass without working.' He has one last idea. To make an observation of the tides.

He ends his happy, solitary life in the simplicity of its days and his own insatiable curiosity. Like Kant in Königsberg, but without the problems with poplar trees or the neighbour's pigeons. He is master of his domain as well as of all he surveys. The view from the terrace of the big square house comprises, to the left, the river mouth and the mountains descending to the water's edge, to the right, kilometres of beach. It is the ideal position from which to study tidal movements in the right angle formed by estuary and sea. He records lunar coordinates and measures low-water marks and coefficients, tidal range, he has graduated scales made and arranges for them to be stuck in mid-current with lamps suspended from their tops. Seated in his rocking chair, notebook on knees, he observes, through navy binoculars, the lights shining in the darkness.

Admiral Decoux, governor general of post-invasion Indochina, living in virtual retirement in Dalat, sends him ephemerides as used in the French navy. Decoux is at a loose end. He has abandoned Puginier Palace in Hanoi to avoid the sight of samurai parading through the city. He and his cabinet are now installed in the Lang Bian Palace, overlooking the Lake. Rather small for an admiral, a lake, something of a comedown. With bombs going off all over the globe and Allied tanks rolling north, having taken Kufra, with kamikaze pilots swooping down on American warships, and with the Red Army, after smashing Germany's Eastern Front, advancing towards Poland, Pétain is confined to Vichy's Park Hotel and Decoux to Dalat's Lang Bian Palace. The French upper crust have pulled back to their spa towns like *curistes* who, come to take the waters, have nothing to do but lounge around beneath marble panelling in dressing gown and slippers. One needs to keep occupied.

Decoux arranges to have the *belle époque* mouldings and decorations adorning the palace stripped out and demolished. He insists on the same being done to the theatre in Saigon's place Francis Garnier, later the National Assembly. Away with all this rococo flab, clearly the work of Jews or Freemasons, it could have dragged France to the edge of the abyss, but for the Marshal. Sharp corners for him, sobriety, Germanic austerity. Just such whims of History, the same sheer blindness, will prompt France, ten years later, to embellish and enlarge the Dalat golf course while the Battle of Dien Bien Phu is being fought. In the expectation that the French staff will want to play a round after their victory. Dalat, the Utopian settlement laid out on the verdant, virgin page of Lang Bian, dreamt of as the possible future capital of all Indochina, is now a lone tiny island that even the Japanese ignore. The admiral paces the palace corridors in a splendid white ceremonial uniform but might as well have stayed in his pyjamas. He frets over his stocks of brandy and champagne, which must be sunk far out in the Lake at the first sight of samurai. As a ship might be scuppered to keep the enemy from seizing it. He knows of Toulon and Mers-el-Kebir. But still the Japanese stay away.

It will be another two years (six months before Hiroshima, six months after the liberation of Paris) before Hirohito's troops, routed on all fronts, launch a furious attack on

French barracks that, after expecting them for five years, have long since dropped their guard. The Japanese slaughter the soldiers and intern the civilians in camps. The locals, playing for time, kowtow by day, keep the Viet Minh informed by night. Wastepaper baskets are searched, so is the admiral's desk, Yersin's recent letter is found, the guerrillas notified that the imperialists are studying the tides, possibly with a view to invading.

Days before his death, Yersin thanks the freshwater admiral for passing on the ephemerides. It is his last letter. 'I shall take the liberty of sending you the findings of these observations in diagram form, once I have collected enough of them.' His eightieth birthday is coming up. He suspects that a celebration is being prepared behind his back. Between binocular watches with his assistant, Tran Quang Xe, he translates his Greeks. His sole posthumous publication will be non-autobiographical: it was Jacotot who gave it one of those post-Rimbaldian titles of which the Pasteurians were so fond: 'Diagrams of tide levels observed at Nha Trang, drawn up from levels recorded by Dr Yersin in front of his Nha Trang house.' He offers it to the *Bulletin of the Society of Indochinese Studies*.

At midnight and six in the morning, then again at six in the evening, Yersin records his observations and fills columns in a notebook that can still be seen in the little museum in

Nha Trang. Occasionally he dozes off. He is not entirely clear what he is doing. Often, dying involves a lot of pain. He knows that from having seen it in hospitals. He floats and drifts in the sound of the waves – aboard a trawler off the Normandy coast, perhaps, or in a first-class cabin, amid the brass trim and varnished wood of the *Oxus* or the *Volga* or the *Saigon*. There is the slow climb up the black swell, a long whisper. The salt water lapping at the mouth of the river, mingling with the fresh. A somnolence, and a very gentle drowning in a strange sadness, rising like the tide. From time to time, a sentence of Pasteur's: 'In the main it finds expression in acts of fermentation and slow combustion, this natural law of dissolution and return to the gaseous state of whatever has once been alive.'

He has himself become the stuff of dreams now. Fishermen light their masthead lamps and sail out to sea. If one of them cuts himself he'll be vaccinated against tetanus, we've got some in the fridge. Tomorrow the fish will gleam on the ice and the prawns will leap in the bottoms of traps. Lights dance on the sea or behind his eyelids. He has another idea. Tomorrow he will eat prawns or perhaps a dandelion salad. He cannot remember – did he in fact think to acclimatise dandelions up at Hon Ba? His thoughts are becoming confused, a creeping flood, the black water swirling and the tide murmuring beneath the moon's great white medallion. The rising water reaching the fuse box in his electrical workshop.

He must activate the circuit breaker, get up, leave his chair. Impossible. Brief flashes from the shorting. The blood vessel bursting in the brain. The time: one in the morning. The light: out.

acknowledgements

My thanks, first of all, go to Professor Alice Dautry, director general of the Paris Pasteur Institute, who kindly allowed me to access the rue Émile Roux archives, to Agnès Raymond-Denise, the curator of those archives, and to Daniel Demellier for help extended in my research as well as for his valuable advice. Also in Paris, my thanks are due to Hoa Tran Huy, Hoan Tran Huy and Minh Tran Huy.

In Morges, to Guillaume Dollmann for looking into the gunpowder industry and for our Ecuadorian trip, following the traces of La Condamine from Quito to Mitad del Mundo.

In Saigon, to my friends Philippe Pasquet and Tran Thi Mong Hong.

In Dalat, to Nguyen Dinh Bong, head of the Pasteur Institute, and to his deputy Dao Thi Vi Hoa.

In Nha Trang, to Truong Thi Thuy Nga, curator of the Yersin Museum at the Pasteur Institute. Also to Tran Dinh Tho Khoi, former student at the Yersin Lycée in Dalat, now a teacher, who acted as my interpreter in those parts as well as with the wardens at Hon Ba, to whom I am likewise grateful for their welcome, their tea and our walk through the forest, with rain beating down, in the footsteps of Yersin.

To buy any of our books and to find out
more about Abacus and Little, Brown, our authors
and titles, as well as events and book clubs,
visit our website

www.littlebrown.co.uk

and follow us on Twitter

**@AbacusBooks
@LittleBrownUK**

To order any Abacus titles p & p free in the UK,
please contact our mail order supplier on:

+ 44 (0)1832 737525

Customers not based in the UK should contact
the same number for appropriate postage
and packing costs.